Long Hot Summer

Long Hot Summer

A Hot Aussie Knights Romance

Victoria Purman

TULE
PUBLISHING

Chapter One

"I THINK WE can turn this into something really special."
Hannie Reynolds held a garish 1970s ring up to the light streaming through the window into her friend's living room. From outside, a calming sea breeze wafted in, and the sounds and smells of an Australian beach summer were evident. The squawk of seagulls. The delighted chatter of children. Cars hovering on the street nearby waiting for that elusive, available car park. The salty tang of fish and chips in the air from a nearby takeaway. Hannie's old friend Beck was lucky enough to live a few steps from the beach at Semaphore, and Hannie had driven down for her cottage in the Adelaide Hills to see Beck and her new baby, Bella.

And to consult.

She stood close to the window, using the light from outside to illuminate a vintage piece of jewellery Beck had recently been given. The stone in the centre, a rose quartz, was badly scratched and had lost its lustre. Set around it was a circle of tiny diamonds, dull now, and the gold band had split at its thinnest part. It appeared to have been abandoned to a jewellery box for more than a few years.

"You really think you can make this old thing into something beautiful?" Beck asked as Bella nuzzled against her breast.

"Oh, most definitely," Hannie replied.

Beck smiled. "That is a relief. I didn't want to be ungrateful when Nana gave it to me, but it's not really me, is it?"

"No, it's not really you, but I'm sure I can turn it into something that you'll love."

Beck was one of Hannie's oldest friends and Hannie knew her tastes. Beck's simple white tank top had a splodge down the front. Her wraparound, tie-dyed skirt skimmed her ankles and she wore a silver ring on her long toe. Her face was bare of makeup, and not just because she'd had a baby just a week before. Beck was an original earth mother, right down to her dreadlocks and her nose ring.

"The stones are really cool, but it's not the kind of thing I would wear, you know?"

Hannie chuckled. "You think?"

"When Nana gave it to me, I was touched, don't get me wrong. It was a beautiful thing for her to do, to celebrate Bella's birth. Her first grandchild and everything. I was thinking you could create something new out of it, something more me, more us, that I can give to Bella when she's older."

Bella gurgled in Beck's arms.

"I can't think of her getting older when she's just been born. Why can't they stay this small and adorable forever?" Hannie walked across the kitchen to Beck, and ran a finger over Bella's smooth cheek, as soft as a feather.

"She is the best thing that's happened to me," Beck sniffed.

Hannie sighed. "Let's make something special to celebrate her arrival, shall we? Is there anything specific you had in mind or would you like want me to work my creative magic and surprise you?"

"Honestly, with the baby brain I have at the moment, I'm going to leave this one all up to you. You know me. I trust you completely. Surprise me."

Hannie thought how lucky she was to have such support from friends like Beck. For years, Hannie had indulged her creative streak by making costume jewellery with chunky resin beads and leather straps, cute rings and earrings and brooches made from old china, as a hobby while she worked in a bank. But in the past eighteen months, her life had changed. She had decided to throw herself into her own business, to see if she could really make a go of it on her own. She'd given up her small house in the inner city and had moved back to the Adelaide Hills to a cottage on her Aunt Mandy's property at Reynolds Ridge, which neighboured the orchard she'd grown up on. The timing of Mandy's offer had been perfect, as the cottage was the perfect size for a new workshop.

Mandy needed a bit of help around the property these days, so the new living arrangements were a match made in Adelaide Hills heaven. Hannie was now her own boss, running a new business repurposing old jewellery, pieces that were once unloved, unfashionable, unwanted, into something fresh and new. She was fulfilled creatively. She loved being near her aunt. She was her own boss and her big old Labrador Ted loved the wide open spaces and the creek at the bottom of the valley. He especially loved the creek when it ran fast and full after the rains.

Hannie slipped Beck's ring into a purple velvet pouch, and tugged at the string to pull it closed it. She slipped it into her workbag.

"I'd love to surprise you. I already have some ideas brewing. Leave it with me." Hannie looped the strap of her workbag over her shoulder. "Now, promise you'll call me if you need anything? I'm totally free to come and sit with Bella while you get some sleep. Or make some of your organic muesli or weave some more hemp clothing. Whatever it is you do in your spare time."

Beck laughed. "I promise."

Before leaving, Hannie made sure to kiss Bella one more time on her delectable, chubby cheeks.

"You be safe up there in the hills," Beck said. "I always worry about you, you know. We're safe down here near the beach, and the sea breezes cool us at night. But... on a hot day, when the winds blow..."

Hannie slipped an arm around Beck's shoulder. "You know me. I'm so prepared I'm like a girl scout. I've done all the fire service training. I have batteries for my portable radio in case we have power outages. I have bottled water and beef jerky stashed away in case of a zombie apocalypse. And you know I grew up on the property right next door. I'm realistic about what it's like up there in summer and the risks."

Beck hugged Hannie. "I know all that in my head. But we both know what high bushfire danger days can be like."

"I'm careful, I promise. I'm prepared to get out early if I have to. I'll just have to make sure I can convince Ted to get in the car with me and we'll be fine."

"How is he doing being cooped up after his knee surgery? I didn't even know that dog's had anterior cruciate ligaments like people do."

The two friends walked down the long hallway out the front door to Hannie's car in the driveway. Beck had Bella in her arms and as they walked, she rocked her from side to side. Hannie opened the passenger door of her car and slung her bag on to the seat.

"And who would have thought they rupture just like humans?" Hannie shook her head in disbelief at what Ted had been through. "He is missing his walks so badly. When I get home, I bet he'll be waiting there in the kitchen with his lead hanging out of his mouth. But he's not supposed to do much of anything until his knee heals. And it's too hot. If I let him wander he'll be in that dry creek bed before I know it, digging up who knows what was buried down there last winter."

Hannie gave Beck one last hug and gave Bella one more kiss. "I'll see you two very soon. When's Mark back from the mines?" Beck's husband worked ten days on and eight days off in the state's mining industry to the north. Hannie didn't know how Beck managed on her own, but she had, for years.

"He's coming home this Friday. I can't wait."

"Give him a kiss from me, will you?"

Beck grinned. "Oh, I will. You drive safe."

ON THE TRIP home, from the beach in the west, up Port Road into the city, Hannie kept a watchful eye on the sky in the distance. It was hot outside, about forty degrees, and she had her car's air-conditioner cranking as high as it would go. Her four-wheel drive had a big cabin and it had heated up sitting in Beck's driveway. At home, in the hills, it was usually cooler, unless a north wind was blowing.

From the Adelaide plains, there was an almost uninterrupted view up to the hills in the east, the ranges purple and light grey and shimmering, the television transmission towers at the highest point, Mt. Lofty, a reference point for the city.

And that uninterrupted view meant Hannie saw the plume of smoke at about the same time it was announced on the radio.

Her heart leapt in her throat. She fired up her Bluetooth

phone to call her Aunt Mandy. She tapped her fingers on the steering while she waited. And waited.

Finally, the call rang out and clicked through to leave a message. "Mandy, it's me. You've probably heard the news. I'm on my way. I'm keeping an eye on it. I've got the radio on in the car and I'm about forty-five minutes away. Call me back."

Her aunt lived in the bigger of two stone houses on the twenty-five hectare property at Reynolds Ridge. Mandy's was a two-storey place, thick-walled and historic, with a heritage listing that recognised its importance to the history of Reynolds' Ridge. It had been an inn in the late nineteenth century, catering to traders crossing the hills and taking goods down into the plains and the city of Adelaide. It was a big place and Mandy rattled around in it, but she didn't want to live anywhere else. Hannie lived in a small stone cottage only a couple of minutes' walk away from the main house. It was a converted barn, with sandstone walls and a restored galvanised iron roof; there were four big rooms inside, one of which was her studio. It was a beautiful part of the world. It was undulating farming country—apples, pears, and cherries, and the orchards and occasional vineyards were surrounded by untamed national parks, which made the entire area vulnerable to fire. Whether started by summer storms and lightning or, unfortunately, arsonists, bushfires were a risk, but they were a price Hannie and her aunt were willing to pay for living where they did.

She took off too fast when a traffic light turned green and had to remind herself to take a deep breath. She didn't have to worry about her aunt. Mandy was probably outside feeding the chooks or getting her goat, Zelda, into her pen. Hannie's septuagenarian aunt had lived in the hills her entire life, knew the precautions one had to take, was sensible enough not to take a risk. But a little thought niggled at Hannie. Mandy's health. While still smart as a whip, and never too shy for a wisecrack aimed at those who perturbed her, she had become physically weaker. While Hannie had noticed her aunt's hands starting to shake, her gait starting to stiffen, the last thing Mandy would do when it came to her own health was listen to her niece, no matter how loved.

"Take a deep breath," Hannie told herself. Mandy would hear the message eventually.

All Hannie had to do was drive across the city and up into the hills, make sure Mandy was safe, check that Ted hadn't chewed everything in the kitchen where she'd block-aded him during his recovery from the surgery, continue listening to the radio, and stay calm. Fires were often caught early and extinguished before they did any major damage. The State's Country Fire Service volunteers, or national park firefighters or even homeowners themselves worked quickly when a fire was reported. And, sometimes, if they were very lucky, a cool change would sweep in and bring clouds laden with rain.

Hannie could only cross her fingers and head for the hills.

HALF AN HOUR later, Hannie hit Reynolds Ridge and, as she drove through the small township, she checked all the shop front windows to see who'd closed up in preparation for being called to go and fight the fires. Many of the locals were volunteers with the Country Fire Service and when their pagers went off, signalling they were needed, they quickly closed up shop, turned off tractors, and stopped whatever else they were doing to get into uniform and hit the trucks.

She was relieved to see A-frame advertising banners still on the footpath and a rainbow flag fluttered outside of Mel and Kaz's Organic Café on the main street. She exhaled. They were all good signs. She slowed, flirting with the idea of pulling in to park on the side of the road and grabbing a coffee, but decided she should get home to see Mandy, since she hadn't been able to reach her on the phone.

That was when she spotted the "For Lease" sign in the shop next door to the café. She checked her rear vision mirror and slowed again so she could get a good look. It was almost like a row cottage, with both premises sharing an adjoining wall, and wrought iron work decorating the corrugated iron veranda like lace on a skirt. It had big front windows, and a door inset from the footpath. She was familiar with the property, but the "For Lease" sign was new.

She shook her head and sighed. It was her dream to have her own shop, a place in which she could combine her workshop with a retail space. She had envisaged it in her head for years—she could decorate the windows with vintage pieces of jeweller's equipment and items she had created. She thought Saturday morning classes for children might also be a way to bring in some extra, steady income.

At this point, her dreams were still dreams. As she accelerated up to the speed limit, she tucked those ideas in the back of her mind.

A few minutes later, Hannie pulled into the property and instead of taking the track to her own cottage, she swung her vehicle sharply left and drove the gravelled driveway to the rear of her aunt's house. Despite her hopes that it might be cooler in the hills, it was scorching and the eucalyptus smell of smoke lingered in the air.

Hannie turned the key and the throaty engine quietened. She leaned across to grab her workbag, opened the door, and closed it behind her.

Which was when she spotted Mandy lying near the back steps, one arm raised in the air, waving weakly.

Her heart skipped a beat. "Oh, god, Mandy." Hannie bolted to her aunt's side. "What on earth have you done?" Hannie looked her over. Mandy was lying on her back on the grass by the back slate steps, one leg raised up and propped gingerly on the lowest rung for elevation.

"I twisted my bloody ankle on the steps. I was watering the pot plants. It's so damn hot they've all wilted. And then, I don't know... I lost my footing and took a tumble. I feel like a damn idiot."

Hannie's stomach plummeted. One more sign that something wasn't right with her aunt.

"Do you hurt anywhere else?" Hannie scanned Mandy from her elevated ankle to her head. She couldn't see any blood on her aunt's face. Her eyes were wide and alert, although there was a wince of pain when Mandy tried to prop herself up by her elbows.

"Don't move," Hannie ordered. She gently pressed a hand to Mandy's shoulder.

"It's just my ankle." Hannie moved to the leg Mandy had propped on the step and gently tugged on her trouser leg, raising it. Above the line of her ankle sock, there was already swelling.

"Okay, I'm going to—"

From behind there was a screech of tyre on gravel. Hannie whipped her head up. A white ute had abruptly come to a halt in the drive and the passenger door whipped open.

"Who's that?" Hannie asked.

It was a man. One with long legs and those long legs were carrying him at great speed, in a few huge strides, to Hannie and her aunt. A baseball cap shadowed his face.

"You okay, Mandy?" He knelt at Mandy's side, studied her face for a moment, and then parted her clenched eyelids so he could check her pupils.

"Who the hell are you?" Hannie demanded.

"You saying you don't remember me?" Man with long legs didn't meet her eyes, but continued to examine Mandy.

"I'm fine, love, really," Mandy tutted.

What the—Hannie's head darted up. She looked across Mandy's prostrate form to the man playing doc with her much-loved aunt.

He took off his baseball cap and shot a quick look in her direction.

His blond hair was short, his jaw strong, and his eyes as blue as the summer sky. When he looked up at her and raised an eyebrow, she felt a shot of something from her toes to her teeth. It was a bigger adrenalin buzz than she'd felt when she'd seen her aunt lying there helpless.

Dylan Knight.

Holy hell.

Chapter Two

"HEY, REYNOLDS," HE smiled. "Long time no see."
Dylan Knight.

The Dylan Knight.

"What… where… why…" Hannie stammered.

"I saw your aunt lying here from my place, up on top of the ridge."

Hannie couldn't speak. What the hell was Dylan Knight doing back in Reynolds Ridge?

And—"Why the hell are you spying on my aunt?" Hannie stood, feet apart, in a fighting stance. Her hands automatically went to her hips, something that wasn't lost on Dylan, judging from the way his eyes dipped.

"Settle down."

She really, really hated when someone told her to settle down, like they thought she was a puppy or something.

He registered the anger on her face and raised his hands in mock defeat. He was still crouched down by Mandy. His thigh muscles bulged inside his jeans. His elbows were perched on his knees and then he returned those his big hands to his examination of Mandy.

"Whoa, take a rain check there before you get all vigilante on me. I was up there at my place on the front deck"—he glanced over his shoulder to the top of Reynolds Ridge—"I had my binoculars out to check my property and all those around the valley, looking for spot fires. I saw Mandy lying here and I jumped in the car. Not stalking, I promise. Not spying, either."

"Right." A wave of relief washed over Hannie.

She looked down at her poor aunt. Wait a second. Her poor aunt seemed to be enjoying this argument with Dylan Knight just a little too much, judging from her wide eyes and the smirk on her face.

"So, is anybody going to help me up?"

"Oh, hell," Hannie exclaimed.

"Damn it," Dylan said at the same time. He then leaned in to Mandy, "Okay if I lift you?"

"Go ahead, handsome," Mandy replied. "I haven't been manhandled by a man in a bloody long time. Make it slow."

And when Hannie glanced from Mandy's cheeky grin to Dylan's face, damn if he wasn't blushing.

When Mandy was upright, Dylan slipped an arm around her waist and half carried, half supported her up the slate steps and across the veranda towards the back door of her house.

"Take her to the living room," Hannie called from close behind, where she tried not to examine Dylan's arse in his jeans. "I'll get some ice."

A couple of minutes later, Mandy was propped up on the sofa, an ice pack on her ankle, chatting with Dylan.

Hannie had gone back to the kitchen and was standing by the sink trying to get her bearings. She stared out the window to the valley, trying to convince herself the shaky feeling that was still thumping through her chest had everything to do with seeing her aunt lying helpless on the ground a few minutes ago and not seeing Dylan Knight again.

What the hell was he doing back in Reynolds Ridge? He'd jumped out of his car like a ghost from her memory, as handsome as ever, still with the same ability to get her pulse thumping and her lady bits wanting all kinds of things. The Knight boys – Dylan and his twin Caleb – had grown up on the property next to her family's, and had enjoyed the notoriety that their genetics created. They weren't identical but were so alike in other ways. Sometimes their hair colour was the only clue for people to hang on to when they were trying to tell which brother was which. Hannie had never been confused about which Knight brother was Dylan. Only one of them had ever been able to get her heart thumping and her pulse racing.

Only one of the Knight boys had kissed her.

Damn her lady bits. Damn her traitorous pulse. Damn him, that Dylan Knight.

All those years of man-crushing she'd done on the boy next door had led to nothing but an unhealthy obsession with Julia Roberts romantic comedies. *Notting Hill*, especially.

Her view from the window, out past Mandy's property, down to the bottom of the valley where the creek flowed when there had been rain, calmed her. The smoke had cleared a little, although she could smell it in the air. Probably would for days. Hannie took a glass from the dish rack, rinsed it, filled it from the tap, and drank it down in huge gulps. Then, she cleaned it and filled it for her aunt. It was important to keep Mandy's fluids up in this heat, especially with an injury. The forecast for the next few days was typically South Australian and summer—hot, damn hot, like the middle of Simpson Desert hot, with forecasts up to forty-four degrees Celsius and overnight lows of a mere twenty-nine degrees. In that moment, like a hundred others during the eighteen months she'd been living on her aunt's property, Hannie was so glad she was close.

Although it now seemed that Mandy had a new guardian angel to look out for her as well as a niece living just a couple of minutes' walk away.

"Hannie," Mandy called out from the living room. "Can you come in here for a minute, love?"

Hannie took a deep breath and turned with the glass of cool water in her hand. She walked around the kitchen table to the living room and, as she appeared in the doorway, Aunty Mandy was smiling up at her. So was Dylan Knight.

She tried not to look at him as she handed the glass of

water to Mandy, who took a small sip.

"C'mon, Aunt Mandy. You'll need more than that. Drink that whole sucker down."

"I know how to drink, you know." Mandy winked at her niece. "Now, Hannie, I was wondering if you could call Alice and let her know what's happened. And, do I have to say it, tell her not to worry?"

"Sure. I'll call her." Hannie flicked a glance at Dylan, tried to ignore the pounding in her chest. "Won't she be pleased to know that a Knight in shining armour arrived just in the nick of time to save the day?"

Mandy laughed. "Oh, you're funny, love. Did you get that, Dylan? A knight in shining armour?"

He frowned "Yeah, she's hilarious."

"I'll call Alice in a minute but first I'll get you some para-cetamol. I think you're going to need it."

A FEW MINUTES later, medication successfully swallowed by her aunt, Hannie was sitting at the kitchen table, talking to her cousin, Alice, on the phone. They were the same age but that was about all they had in common. Alice had never liked that her mother had invited Hannie to move into the cottage on her property. Not that she'd ever come out and said exactly that, but Hannie knew. The simple fact was that Alice didn't trust her. Not after what had happened at the end of year party in their final year of high school. It had been fourteen years ago, but still Alice bore a grudge.

And Hannie still felt the guilt.

"She's fine, Alice. Someone came to help her just as I got home."

Please don't ask who the someone is. Please don't.

"Someone came to help her? Where were *you*?"

Settle down. Don't bite back. Hannie had to believe Alice was actually worried about her mother more than she wanted to make Hannie feel guilty.

"I was with a client down at Semaphore. I was on my way home when I saw the smoke in the hills and I came right here. We're all safe. I haven't had time to flick on the radio to see what the latest reports are, but the smoke has dissipated and the wind has dropped."

"There was a fire?" Alice sounded horrified. For someone who'd grown up in the very house Mandy still lived in, one would think Alice had never heard of the bushfire season.

"Look, Alice, she's good. She can put weight on her ankle so I think it's just a sprain. She's resting with ice on it."

"I can't believe you haven't got her in the car right now and taken her to hospital." Alice said. "Honestly, Hannie, what is the point of you freeloading on my family if you're not even going to look after her at times like this?"

Hannie clamped her lips shut. She shouldn't say out loud what was sitting in the top of her tongue. Oh, but she wanted to. "If I thought she needed it, Alice, she would be in hospital right now and you know it. Why don't you come up and see for yourself? I'm sure she'd love to see you."

There was hesitation down the line.

Alice cleared her throat. "Well, of course, I know she'd like that, but it's almost school pick up time and I have to go and pick up the kids. It'll only upset Mum if she thinks we've rushed up from town to check on her. Perhaps it's best if I don't."

No, of course you're not coming. Hannie didn't want to count how many months it had been since Alice had made the twenty minute trip into the hills from her lovely home in the city to visit her mother. There was always an excuse— Natasha's soccer practice or Ainslie's theatre group. A very important work dinner or her husband's travel. Hannie had always thought Alice was selfish and self-centred, but how could a daughter not visit her mother? If Hannie's mother, Lucy, was still in the same state, Hannie would be the kind of daughter who would visit twice a week, at least. Especially for dinner. No one cooked like her mother. As it was, Hannie managed to get to far North Queensland, more than three thousand kilometres away – a three hour flight – once a year. When Lucy's husband had died, only a year after they'd married, she'd decided to sell up everything and move to a place where there were no bushfires.

"Tropical cyclones I can handle," her mother had said when she'd announced her decision to move to Cairns. "But not another fire. I simply can't do it, Hannie."

Hannie couldn't argue. When Hannie's mother had lost

her husband – Hannie's stepfather – in a fire, she had been devastated. The newly-married couple had only had two years together when he died.

Hannie tried to concentrate on what Alice had said. Oh yeah, the fact that Alice didn't want to rush up and see her own mother.

"I'll let you know if anything changes," Hannie said. "I promise."

"I'll ring her later."

The cousins ended the call. Hannie crossed her arms on the kitchen table and flopped her head down on them. She felt tired. It must have been the adrenaline rush or maybe the heat or the smoke. This jittery feeling had nothing to do with the fact that Dylan Knight was in the next room. No, nothing at all.

"Hey."

She jerked her head up. Okay, so not in the next room. In this room. With her.

"Were you talking to Alice?"

"Yes."

The mere mention of her name clouded the atmosphere between them. Dylan's frown returned and Hannie couldn't bear to see it on his handsome face.

His voice was businesslike suddenly. "I hope you told her there's nothing to worry about. I've got Mandy all propped up on the sofa with a couple of pillows under that ankle. It's not broken. She's got a mild sprain, but it probably shook her up."

Dylan swaggered over to the table and pulled out a chair. Dylan Knight didn't simply walk anywhere. He spun the chair around and sat on it backwards, his elbows on the back rest.

"Maybe I should take her to hospital," Hannie said, trying to stare at the grainy lines of the pine table and not his eyes. She glanced up quickly. Come to think of it, his hair was the same golden yellow as the table.

Oh, crap.

"If you want, sure. But I've checked her out. It's a sprain."

"But what if you're wrong? What if it's broken?"

"News flash. One of the first things you learn when you go to firefighter school is all the boring first aid. You know, like sprains and broken bones and heart attacks and delivering babies. That stuff."

"Yeah, of course." She hesitated. "You've delivered a baby?"

"Once or twice." He shrugged. "But go ahead and take her to hospital if you want to."

Hannie finally looked him in the eye. She couldn't share her suspicions about Mandy with anyone, especially not him. "If I even suggested that, she'd bite my head off."

"Yeah, I figured that. Paracetamol and ice."

"Right. Paracetamol and ice. I can do that. I mean, I'm no first responder or anything, but even I can manage that."

He smiled at her. Little lines at the corners of his eyes crinkled. His teeth were very white against his tanned face.

"So. How long have you been back?" Hannie asked.

"A month."

"A month?" She hadn't noticed lights on in the house across the valley. She hadn't seen him around. Not at the café. Or on the road. Not across the valley looking lovelorn in her direction. It wasn't like Reynolds Ridge was a thriving metropolis. Puff. Her spidey sense hadn't tingled once at his proximity the way she thought it might have.

Maybe she really was over him.

That would be good. It would be very good. It would be entirely excellent.

But here he was in her aunt's kitchen and something was definitely tingling. Perhaps it was her guilt pinging back to life.

"I hadn't planned on coming back from Melbourne but when Mum and Dad didn't like any of the offers they had for the property... I got a convenient case of homesickness."

"And you bought the property?"

"Yep."

"Caleb didn't want it?"

"Yep. He did. But I wanted it more."

"Oh." Hannie knew what he was talking about.

He couldn't bear to let the place go, to be sold into another family, to end his family's history and connection with this area. Her family and his had been neighbours since they were kids, and their families before them. Four generations of Knights and Reynolds had lived alongside each other. She knew from her mother that Dylan's father hadn't been well after a heart attack two years ago, when he'd had to retire from the fire service, and Dylan's purchase of the property was about securing the future of his parents in a retirement village, closer to medical care in somewhere more manageable.

"How are they enjoying life in the retirement village?"

His smile widened. "It's a nice place. Not far from here. Dad makes a big show of hating the place, of course. But Mum loves it. Probably because she's not stuck with him twenty-four hours a day. She gets to do things like Zumba dancing and Thai cooking classes and the place has a tennis court and a pool."

"That sounds nice," Hannie said. "I'm sure he'll come around."

"Yeah, he will. As long as they're together, he'll be happy."

There was something unspoken, though, in his explanation. She knew how much his parents would be missing Reynolds Ridge—the foggy winter mornings, the winter chill, the open fires, the bursts of spring leaves in the trees and the cooling gully breezes in summer. The view out across the apple orchards and the crisp clean scent of an autumn morning. That was exactly what she'd missed when she'd moved away. They didn't have a choice to leave though and, it seemed, Dylan didn't have one about coming back.

"So you're back…" Her voice trailed off. She really wanted to keep going to ask him if he was back for good, but stopped herself. It really was none of her business, no matter how much traitorous tingling was going on inside her.

"Yep. For good."

"And you're back in the South Australian fire service?" It was a casual question.

"Yep. Back on the trucks," he said, distracted.

"Well. Welcome home, Dylan Knight."

She met his eyes. He did nothing for a moment. He simply stared back at her.

And, oh, god. She was back in the school hall and he was about to kiss her.

Then her phone beeped and vibrated on the table. She glanced down. It was a message from Alice. She felt hot and nauseous all of a sudden.

"Please make sure Mum keeps her leg elevated"

Hannie blew out a breath.

"What's the matter? Who's that?"

Hannie met his eyes when she said, "It's Alice."

Dylan's back straightened.

Your first love, Alice. The one we betrayed.

A heavy silence descended, thicker than the smoke from any bushfire.

"Well," she said.

"Well." Dylan stood, flipped the chair around and tucked it under the table. "I'd better get going."

"Sure." Hannie grabbed her phone, stood to tuck it into her pocket. "Ice and paracetamol."

"Ice and paracetamol. And make sure she keeps it elevated for the rest of the day."

Hannie flicked a pointed finger at him. "You don't need to tell me twice."

"No," he said gruffly. "I'm sure I don't. I'll get going."

Hannie tapped her skull. "Up here for thinking." Then she pointed to her feet. "And down here for dancing."

She froze. *Dancing.* Why the hell did she have to mention that?

Dylan didn't move. He just stood there in her aunt's kitchen, his feet planted, his head close to the ceiling of the old cottage. "It's good to see you, Hannie."

"You too," she replied with a forced smile.

He dipped his head in goodbye, then turned and walked out the back door. A moment later, the rumble of his car starting echoed in the valley and the sound of it faded as he drove out the long driveway onto the main road.

Chapter Three

H ANNIE MADE A quick trip to her cottage. She had to cuddle Ted, make sure he had enough water and let him outside for a pitstop and a quick sniff around the yard. Then, she returned to her Aunt Mandy's place. She'd been visiting a lot more lately, as her concerns had continued to grow. After dinner, they watched a Rambo movie on DVD—her aunt had had a thing for Sylvester Stallone since the 1970s—then Hannie helped Mandy get in to bed, and left after promising to return in the morning to see that she could get up and about and keeping up with the paracetamol and fluids.

Closing the back door behind her, Hannie stepped down from the veranda and slowly walked the driveway to her own cottage. It was a quiet night. The stars were putting on a twinkling show in the sky and, with few street lights in the hills, there was no city glare to distract from their brightness. There was rustling in the big oak tree by the drive way, and the familiar call of a boobook owl was reassuring. If the birds hadn't flown away, it felt safe.

It had been a long day. Semaphore that morning with Beck and Bella. The smoke. Mandy. Dylan.

Hannie sighed. If she had a bath tub, she would have filled it to the brim and added scented bubbles to soak in it for about four hours. But she didn't, so when she pushed open her front door, she headed straight to the bathroom for a cooling shower before slipping into bed.

Most nights, the gully breezes cooled her cottage, slipping in through the tall living room windows and exiting from her bedroom windows, fluttering the net curtains all night in a pretty dance. But tonight it was still. And still hot. At least Hannie was using the heat as an excuse for her inability to sleep. She turned on one side, then the other. Flicked off the thin sheet covering her, then scrabbled around on the floor looking for it when she felt cool.

She checked her bedside clock. It was one a.m. It was no use. She was way too revved up to sleep. And she had to admit it had about ten percent to do with what had happened to her aunt and ninety percent to do with Dylan.

Dylan Knight. The boy next door. Well, from the property next door to be absolutely correct. Dylan, his brother, Caleb and Alice and Hannie had grown up within two kilometres of each other, the edges of their family's properties meeting at a point deep in the gully under Reynolds Ridge. The Knights and the Reynolds had been in the area for generations; an uncle four generations ago had named the ridge after himself, so every generation since had claimed a connection with the area. All three families had been in-volved in the same community organisations, the same fundraising drives for the local fire service, the local hospital, and they had all gone to high school together.

Which was where Dylan Knight had taken one look at Alice, standing in the line at the school cafeteria, flicking her long blonde ponytail in a graceful arc as she swivelled to avoid his eye, and had been smitten. Hannie had seen it with her own eyes. Not that she hung around with Alice at school, even thought they were cousins and had grown up together. She and Alice had inhabited vastly different teenaged worlds. Hannie had spent her lunchtimes in the library because it was easier than trying to make friends, and Alice had spent her lunch times sauntering around the school yard revelling in her power and popularity.

Alice had been the "It Girl". She was born beautiful and charming and just… well, everything she'd ever done was just perfect. And, without saying it, the kids at school had given up their power to her. If Reynolds Ridge High had been a 1980s movie with Molly Ringwald in it, Alice would have been the "Queen of the Teens". Her hair was always just the right blonde and so smooth. She always had lots of friends and was invited to parties every weekend. Hannie was, by contrast, the geeky library kid who continually pushed her glasses up her nose. Except there had never been a magical movie makeover for Hannie in the final reel. She had continued to be geeky, book-obsessed, and mostly friendless, until she started her first job and met Beck. They had immediately sensed something alternative about each other and, finally, Hannie had found a friend.

Alice's high school years had been blessed by having won Dylan's attention. They were the perfect couple. By contrast, Hannie had spent her whole high school life feeling invisible to the boy she was secretly in love with.

She was worse than the girl next door to him. She was the kid next door. So she'd tried not to stare. Tried not to cry when she saw characters on TV shows named Dylan. Tried to develop gigantic crushes on other boys like that sweet guy Trevor Haines from her class, but it had all been in vain.

That night of the party, when they were all about to go their separate ways after high school, she'd tried not to overreact when Dylan had asked her to dance.

He was being kind to her because he felt sorry for her, because no one else had asked her and it was the last time they would all be together and they'd been neighbours forever and he was being the nice boy next door, that was all.

Hannie hadn't really started to fall out of love with Dylan Knight until the moment Alice had caught them, her face in his hands, his lips on hers, her hands around his waist, clinging to him as the thrill of her first kiss had vibrated in every part of her. Hannie still heard Alice's screams and accusations in her head when she imagined that moment.

Dylan had torn his lips from hers, sworn under his

breath, then grabbed Alice's hand and taken her outside to calm down. The next week, he'd left for Melbourne and Hannie hadn't seen him since.

And now, fourteen years later, he was back. He wasn't that teenage boy anymore, oh no. He'd grown into his height and his shoulders were far broader than she'd imagined. And he didn't have adult crinkles around his eyes back then.

As for Hannie, she'd drifted between jobs until she'd found her passion in jewellery making. Except for a short stint living in the city because it was something she thought she should do, she had always remained connected to Reynolds Ridge. She knew these roads and tracks like the freckles on the back of her hand.

And now Dylan was back and Alice was close by.

Hannie hadn't noticed a ring on his finger the night before when they'd been chatting around the kitchen table. Although that didn't mean anything. She wore a ring on the ring finger of her left hand – one of her own, of course – and she wasn't married. Had never been married. Had had a boyfriend for five years in her twenties. She'd broken up with him just after he'd proposed marriage. The problem was she couldn't imagine a future with Andrew, no matter how lovely he was.

Hannie kicked off the sheets. The glowing clock reminded her that it was way too late to be tossing and turning. What was she – sixteen again? No. She was double that age now. She was thirty-two years old. Thirty-two sensible years old. Too old to be feeling like a lovesick teenager.

She had to get a grip. She stomped out of bed to go to the toilet. When she reached the kitchen, she stopped to pat Ted. He was stretched out on the slate tiled floor, and didn't move, except for his tail which thumped a dull rhythm. She didn't like confining him to the kitchen, but it was on the vet's strictest orders.

"Listen now, Ted," she'd said when Hannie had picked him up the day after his surgery. "No running around. You let that knee heal, you hear?" So Hannie had to confine him on a long leash to stop him from bolting out of the house and heading up to Mandy's for a treat. He was one smart dog.

And he was her best friend.

He was all the distraction she needed right now. Him and Mandy. She had no room in her life to be diverted by a pair of fine arms and a smile so warm it melted her insides like a blow torch. She couldn't go back to wanting Dylan because with the wanting came the guilt for what they'd done.

She had a life now, one she loved, and she wasn't going to let it be thrown off balance by the return of Dylan Knight.

DYLAN SAT ON his front balcony, cradling a whiskey in his hands. His bare feet were propped up on the wooden railing and he'd slouched back in a canvas deck chair, angling himself so the stars were all he could see. The sting in the heat of the day had left with the sunset, and he sat patiently waiting for a hint of gully breeze. He arched his neck. Was that it? There was the faintest rustle in the leaves in the gums surrounding his property and it stirred memories, too.

"You'll sleep fine tonight with that breeze," his father had always said when he'd thrown open the windows after a scorching summer's day. "Let the outside in."

He'd forgotten this view, how beautiful Reynolds Ridge was. The apple and cherry orchards were laid out before him like a pinstripe suit, in straight and organised lines up and down the valley; nearby, the national park, home to birds and 'roos and koalas. He hadn't realised how much he'd missed it until he'd come home. When he'd moved to Melbourne fourteen years before, he'd lived in the city while he undertook his training and had then worked at a suburban station, tackling house fires and vehicle accidents and oil spills and businesses up in flames. When the devastating bushfires had hit Victoria a few years back, he'd volunteered along with hundreds of his colleagues, trying to save properties and lives. He'd been glad to get back to his station after that. The city seemed safer after what he'd seen.

But duty – and family – had called him home to Adelaide. His folks needed him, and some people who weren't twins would think it was weird, but he liked being closer to his brother, Caleb. The last time he'd seen him had been two weeks before, at their grandfather's funeral in Brisbane. Len Knight, a man who had been Australia's chief fire officer and the patriarch of a fire fighting family which spanned states and nations, had died suddenly of a heart attack. Some thought he'd died with a broken heart; a heart crushed by attempts to blame him for all that went wrong during the devastating fires in Victoria a few years before. Dylan didn't know what was true. All he knew was that his grandfather was dead, and his grandmother was now a widow. The entire clan had gathered for his funeral to honour and remember him; to reflect on the legacy of the man who had inspired all of them to remember that there was strength in unity.

Dylan and Caleb had flown up to BrisVegas together and, in a pact after the funeral, the two of them, along with their cousins Logan and Dare, had honoured their grandfather in the best way they knew how.

Dylan glanced at his left bicep. The tattoo was still raised and red and a little tender. It said, in cursive script, "Brothers forged in fire."

He shook his head. It was such a fucking stupid thing to have done, but the memory of it, the camaraderie of doing that fucking stupid thing with his brother and their cousins, made him grin. He glanced at his watch. It was one a.m. Too late to ring Caleb and stir the shit out of him over the damn tattoos. He remembered that Caleb was on early shift this week and wouldn't wake him just to talk.

Something caught his eye from across the valley. A light

flicked on at Hannie's place.

Hannie Reynolds. Wasn't she a surprise?

It had been a long time. High school. That was the last time he'd seen her. Yeah, that night of the party. How could he forget?

As he searched the sky for the stars of the Southern Cross, he tried to decide what it was about Hannie now that had him thinking about her, sitting out here in the dark. If he should be thinking of any woman, wouldn't it be Alice? But he wasn't thinking about Alice. He'd got over Alice the day he'd broken up with her, a week before that party. They'd been together as kids, then young adults and when she'd pushed and pushed about going to Melbourne with him, to be there by his side when he was training, he had to end it. She wanted a fantasy about being the perfect couple with a perfect life.

He'd realised his fantasy was about someone else.

Hannie Reynolds.

The kid from the property next door. The first time he'd really become aware of her was the football incident.

It had been winter, and he and Caleb had some mates from high school over to kick the football around. Their school team had won their game the day before and, fuelled by dreams that they might all get to play for a national side when they were a little older, they spent hours out in the low paddock, kicking that damn football to each other, kicking goals between an old tree stump and a young gum sapling.

The back fence was the boundary and out of bounds meant whoever kicked the ball had to scramble down into the mud of the creek to retrieve it.

He'd kicked another goal and instead of landing in the creek, the football had soared over it into the Reynolds' property and into the branches of a scrabbly gum. When he'd looked over, he'd seen Hannie standing in the tall, green grass.

"Hey, Reynolds," he'd called. He'd cupped his hands around his mouth so his voice could carry across the creek. "The ball. It's in that tree."

She'd looked up into the branches. She stuffed something in the pocket of her big, puffy jacket and then walked over to the tree, reached up and shaken the branch. The faded red oval-shaped ball had fallen and she'd expertly caught it. Dylan had been jogging closer to the creek, anticipating she would throw it over to him. He was twenty feet away, the creek and the barbed wire between them.

But damn if Reynolds didn't throw the ball back to him. She'd moved away from the gum tree, giving herself a straight line across to Dylan's parents' property. She held the ball in her hands, dead in front of her. She took a step, then another, then starting into a slow jog and in a smooth motion he'd seen a thousand times but never from a girl, she dropped the ball on to her foot and kicked the hell out of that red leather. Dylan's eyes had lifted as the ball soared into the sky, cherry red against the winter clouds, and it turned over and over, long end over long end, way over Dylan's head. When it landed thirty feet beyond him, he heard his mates start cheering. They'd quickly snatched up the ball and kicked a goal at the other end of their makeshift oval.

Dylan didn't turn to see what was going on with the game.

It was a long moment before he raised a hand, a wave to say thanks. She had given him the slightest of nods and turned back to the house. He wished he'd complimented her on that kick. These days, a young girl could turn a kick like that into a professional football career.

But Hannie wasn't that young girl anymore. The black hair she'd always worn short and punky, with a rainbow of colours streaked through it, was now long and curly, swept up on top of her head in a loose kind of ponytail. There was a calmness about her that had been reassuring, given what had happened to her aunt. She wasn't a hothead, Hannie, or a panicker or a drama queen. Mandy was in good hands.

Which made him think of her hands, long and elegant, and the jewellery she'd been wearing. Two big, fat chunky rings, one on each middle finger, in unusual designs with a black stone in each.

He pulled himself up. He'd been there – what – half an hour – and he'd managed to take in all this detail about Hannie Reynolds from next door?

Nah, he wasn't interested. Not *interested* interested. She was someone he'd grown up with that was all. Someone from the good old days. The older he got, the more nostalgic he felt about people he'd gone to school with and grown up around. Like Trevor from the next town who was now Tania. Suzie, the shy girl from the school drama productions, who was now making films in Hollywood. Pete and Amanda, high school sweethearts who he'd run into in the local supermarket, who were blissfully happy parents to six kids. He was interested in that kind of stuff.

His mind went back to the party and that kiss. Their first. Their only. That night, he'd realised how much time he'd wasted being with the wrong girl. So he'd done something impetuous and stupid. He'd kissed the right girl. And it wasn't just his memory playing tricks on him. Hannie had kissed him right back. She'd opened her mouth and flicked her tongue against his, wrapped her arms around his waist and pressed herself against him.

Then Alice had screamed across the school hall and Hannie had frozen in his arms.

"Hannie Reynolds! What the fuck are you doing?"

He'd called Hannie the next day before he'd left, leaving three messages, but she didn't ever call him back. And she hadn't answered his emails, either.

No, he wasn't interested in Hannie Reynolds. They were neighbours once more, it seemed. And that was all they would be.

While he'd broken up with Alice on terms that were hardly friendly, he'd always liked her mother. He was relieved Mandy hadn't been seriously injured in the fall on her front steps. He'd always liked her and now, older and wiser, her plain-speaking, no-nonsense manner made him wonder where Alice's ambitious attitudes had come from.

Hannie shared some of the same DNA as her cousin but she wasn't anything like Alice.

He upended his glass and swallowed the whiskey down. He stood, leaned over the railing. In the distance, lights from the little stone cottage at the bottom of the valley twinkled.

Then they flicked off and it was dark.

The stars above glowed bright in the summer night sky.

His mind drifted back to something his cousin Logan had said at their grandfather's wake. They'd been drinking to his memory when Logan had piped up and said, "To getting laid and fighting fires."

The fire fighting part of this life was taken care off.

Dylan decided he should probably check on Mandy tomorrow. See if she was okay, it she was keeping up the ice and the paracetamol. And if he happened to run into Hannie when he was doing that? He was a professional firefighter. He could handle anything.

Chapter Four

HANNIE PULLED HERSELF closer to her jeweller's table and slipped on her magnifying glasses. Double lensed with very high magnification, they looked like something out of a steampunk costume exhibition, and they were the perfect tool to get a really close look at the stones in Beck's grandmother's ring.

There was a whimper from her feet. She looked down.

"You want a pat, huh?" She leaned down and rubbed Ted's ears, then reached for the small ceramic bowl she kept on her table which contained small pieces of dried liver treats. She flipped one in the air and Ted expertly snatched it.

That would keep her hound happy for a little while, so she returned to her examination and as she rotated the piece, catching the light in the carats, she tried to imagine what she could create. A brooch, perhaps? A pendant for Beck's daughter, Bella, to wear when she was older?

Nothing came to mind. She couldn't settle her thinking. Usually, she could slip on her glasses and immerse herself in her work, in the fine filigree and the stones and the gold and silver. Something was off today. She tried a new approach. She put the stones down, leaned back in her chair, closed her eyes and tried to let her imagination take over. It helped when she was designing. She always started in her mind's eye, not on paper. She tried to see the refraction of the light; tried to decide – gold or silver – and tried to match a piece with the personality of its prospective owner. Were they traditional? Quirky? Minimalist or housewives of New Jersey?

Beck sat firmly in the quirky category but there was no way to know what her daughter would be like. Quirky sometimes skipped a generation, didn't it? Alice and Mandy were a perfect example of that. Mandy was all country calm and practicality, no-nonsense with a wit like a razor. Alice was haughty, stifled, pretentious, and tense. Hannie couldn't remember her cousin ever cracking a joke.

Ted growled and sat upright. Hannie glanced down at him and then heard footsteps.

"Hey."

Her jeweller's glasses made everything look stretched out of proportion and fuzzy but she didn't need to see clearly to know it was Dylan.

She whipped off her glasses, placed them on her desk, and turned back to him.

She squinted, rubbed her eyes, and shook her head.

"You okay?"

"Yeah, I'm fine. It's just takes me a minute to focus after wearing these things." She narrowed her eyes and Dylan was standing before her, his face a picture of concern. She waved him away, tried not to look at his sky blue eyes.

"No need for first aid here, firefighter Knight. I'm fine. What are you doing here?"

"I was just up to Mandy's to see how she is. I thought I'd stop by."

Two visits in two days. Mmm. Maybe he'd been hoping that Alice was there visiting her mother with a fruit basket or something. Hannie knew the chance of that were slim to nonexistent.

"She seemed good this morning when I was up there for breakfast," Hannie said. "She wolfed down the scrambled eggs and bacon I made for her. And three pieces of toast."

Dylan chuckled. "If I'd known that I wouldn't have just left her with a cherry pie."

Hannie gasped. "Are you talking about a cherry pie from Mel and Kaz's Organic Café on the main road through Reynolds Ridge?"

"Aren't they the best?"

"Oh, god, they're to die for."

Dylan crossed his arms and chuckled. "If I'd known you were such a foodie, I would have brought you one, too."

"Thanks, but, while they're delicious, a whole pie is wasted on me."

He narrowed his eyes playfully. "What makes you think

I'd let you eat it all by yourself?"

Was he flirting with her? She smiled at the floor.

"And who's this?" Dylan crouched down and held out a hand to Ted. It didn't take a moment for her fearless guard dog to be licking Dylan's hand as if it were smothered in one of Ted's favourite things—dead birds or his own vomit.

"Ted. And before you ask it's not short for anything like Edward or Theodore. He's just Ted."

"Why's he leashed up like this?" Dylan rustled the long leash that was looped around the leg of Hannie's desk.

"See that shaved patch on his left hind leg? He's had an anterior cruciate ligament repair. He's not allowed to run until it's properly healed."

"Mate," Dylan said with concern, "you poor bastard." Ted flipped over on to his belly and gratefully accepted the scratch he received.

"Would you like a coffee, Dylan? I have one of those fancy capsule machines if that floats your boat."

"Sure. I'd love one." He stood, a move which created a whimper of disappointment from Ted, and took a step closer to Hannie's desk. "What's all this? What are you making?"

Hannie half-swivelled back to her desk as he moved closer. He looked over her tools, the half-moon cutout of the front edge of her tall desk, her high wattage lamp, her tray full of stones and old pieces. As he did, he absentmindedly scratched Ted behind an ear.

"I make jewellery. Or, more specifically, I create new

pieces out of old ones."

"Really?" Dylan looked back over his shoulder at her. "Upmarket recycling, huh?"

"Yeah, you could say that."

He picked out a stone from her tray and held up under the lamp. "This is a sapphire, right?"

She moved forward to see what he was holding, accidentally bumping her shoulder against his hip. Her tingling alert dialled up to eight.

"Yep. It's an Australian sapphire, actually."

"No kidding? I thought they were all from Ceylon... Or should I say, Sri Lanka."

"Sapphires have been mined in Australia for more than one hundred years, mostly on the New South Wales Tablelands around Inverell."

"Well," Dylan carefully placed the stone back in its tray and turned to her. "You learn something every day. You're a jeweller."

"And you're a firefighter."

"Yep."

"Well," Hannie said. "Haven't we grown up then?"

His eyes took a slow journey down her body. "Yes, we have. This isn't high school anymore."

Oh no. The tingles were moving up her body and now her tongue felt thick. She cleared her throat. "How about that coffee?" She took off without waiting for an answer, ducking her head to pass through the low doorway in the thick stone wall, down the hallway, her bare feet padding on the cool slate tiles, and turned left into the kitchen.

Cursing herself, she filled the water well on her coffee pod machine before slipping in a pod at the top.

"How do you have it, Dylan?"

"Black. Thanks."

Hannie stared at the gurgling coffee machine.

"Who's in Cairns?"

Hannie turned to see Dylan studying the postcard collection on her fridge. "Mum. She likes to send me postcards of where she lives now, in a barely-concealed attempt to lure me up there more regularly."

"It's a beautiful part of the world, although, obviously, not as great as Reynolds Ridge. Do you get up there to see her often?"

"I fly up once a year and she comes back once a year. I wish it could be more but, you know, a gal's gotta make a living to afford expensive flights like that."

"She must miss you," Dylan said. "It must be hard for her to have her daughter so far away."

His observation pulled her up. "It's hard for me too, but you know, we Skype. And I have Mandy to fuss over."

Dylan looked around the room. "This is a great place. I remember it the way it was back in the day. No roof, a pile of old sandstone, weeds as high as your waist. Remember? We used to think it was haunted."

"You used to think it was haunted. I never believed that

claptrap."

Dylan laughed. "Oh, that is total bullshit. You were totally scared of this place."

"Was not."

"You were too. I distinctly remember poking around in here with you and Alice and you getting a fright and running back up the hill. You were white as a ghost."

Hannie froze. He was right. But it wasn't a ghost that had stolen the breath from her lungs. That had been the first time she'd seen Dylan and Alice kissing. She'd turned a corner into one of the old rooms and they'd been standing with their arms around each other, lips firmly locked. Hannie could still feel the cool, crumbling sandstone under her fingers as she'd run her hands along the wall, steadying herself so she didn't tumble on the fallen stones hidden under the long grass at her feet.

Hannie gave Dylan his coffee.

"Thanks." He took a sip. "So, there's a story here."

"A story about what?"

"About why you're living on Mandy's property."

It wasn't that complicated, but Hannie suddenly felt shy about sharing her life story with Dylan. The reasons why were sad and complicated and brought back too many memories.

She hesitated. "When Mum's husband died... she couldn't stay here in Reynolds Ridge."

Dylan put his cup on the table, came closer. "Oh hell, he

died in a bushfire, didn't he? Two years ago."

Hannie nodded. She studied her bare feet, felt the cool of the slate warm under her toes. When she looked up, craning her neck to meet his eyes, she saw something surprising. Tenderness. Concern. And then he reached a hand out and rested it on her bare shoulder, where the strap of her singlet top bared her skin.

"I'm so sorry. That must have been... well, I don't need to tell you what it was like for you and your mum."

She swallowed and took a deep breath in. "After what happened, after what she went through, Mum moved to north Queensland. She sold off the property which meant I had to move to the city, until Mandy invited me to come back. She'd done up the cottage by then, and was renting it out, but she became wary of having strangers living on her property. And, I needed a studio, so we did each other a favour, really."

His grip on her shoulder tightened. His eyes moved from her to her mouth. She felt suddenly parched.

"And Mandy needs someone to keep an eye on her, doesn't she?"

"She's not exactly a spring chicken any more, I know that, but she's pretty independent."

"That's not what I mean, Hannie." He'd seemed to have forgotten to take his hand of her shoulder.

"I don't know what you're talking about."

His chest rose and fell. "Her injury. Tripping on the

front steps. What else have you noticed?"

Hannie closed her eyes. How did he know? In the eighteen months she'd been living on her aunt's property, she'd seen the signs. She'd increasingly been doing more, when her aunt was unable to, but whenever Hannie had tried to raise the subject of her health, Mandy had flatly refused to discuss it.

"I'm an old woman. And I'll be a grumpy old woman if you keep nagging me about seeing a doctor."

And that had been the end of the discussion. So Hannie had tried not to notice her aunt's shaking hands, the tremor in her voice, her increasing tiredness.

"IS IT PARKINSON'S?"

Hannie felt weak at the knees. "Parkinson's?" Her voice echoed around the stone walls of her studio. "I don't know, Dylan. I'm not a doctor. She won't tell me anything. She flatly refuses to discuss it and I've been scared to push it with her."

Hannie pushed him back, away from her, her palm on his T-shirt, on his chest. She couldn't seem to find any words.

"How long since you've noticed things haven't been quite right?"

Hannie covered her mouth with a hand, as if saying it out loud would make it real. "Twelve months. A bit more. It was her birthday before last and I noticed her hand shaking when she was cutting the cake. Alice was too busy running around after her kids to notice. But I noticed."

"You don't think she's told anybody?"

Hannie shook her head.

"Not even Alice?"

A cold shiver settled in her chest. "No. Not even Alice."

He took his hand away, stepped back. She dropped hers.

"Are you telling me that Mandy hasn't told her own daughter that she's sick?"

"No."

"What the hell is all that about?"

Hannie but her lip in frustration. How on earth could she tell Dylan the truth about the relationship between Mandy and her own daughter? For years, Hannie had been caught in the middle, a keeper of Mandy's secrets, a bulwark against Alice's bullying opinions and Mandy's stubborn intransigence.

"That's between them. I've spent my whole life trying to figure them out and I can't so I don't try. But you can't say anything to either of them. Do you understand?"

Dylan shook his head. She could see the frustration in his face.

"If it was one of my parents, I'd want to know."

Of course he would. He'd come home at the drop of a hat to buy his parents' property when they had to sell up.

"Me, too," Hannie said.

He ran a hand through his blond hair, ruffling it.

"I can't say I understand any of this shit, but you have my word. I won't say anything."

From outside, a gusty, scorching wind invaded Hannie's studio, swirled around the room, catching her hair and teasing it across her face. A pile of papers on a sideboard were swept up and tumbled to the floor.

"Oh, shit." She scooped them up and clutched them to her chest.

"It's another bad fire day today," Dylan said.

"Isn't every day a bad fire day in Adelaide in February?"

Dylan reached down behind him for a stray piece of paper and passed it to her. She gathered it with her others.

He paused, looked around the room. "Well, I'd better be heading back."

"Thanks for checking on Mandy." Hannie could see in his face how much he cared for Mandy. If Hannie hadn't kissed him that night, he might have been her son-in-law now instead of an old neighbour.

"I'm glad she's okay." Dylan reached down to give Ted a final scratch, then walked to the doorway, ducking his head to make it under.

"See you."

He took a step back and looked over his shoulder. "Bye."

When she was sure he'd gone out the front door, Hannie moved to the window of her studio, and watched Dylan walk up towards her aunt's house where his car was parked. It felt as if he was walking out of her life.

And perhaps that was for the best.

Hannie pulled the old sash window closed.

THE WIND FELT more dangerous as the morning wore on and became midday—menacing, fierce with heat and ferocious in its speed. Hannie didn't like days like this but had learned to bear them. She'd had almost thirty two summers up here at Reynolds Ridge, alive to the possibility of fleeing at a moment's notice. She and Mandy were fully prepared to get in the car and get out if the fire experts said so. The Bureau of Meteorology forecasters and the emergency broadcaster were a lifeline during the summer months. Hannie knew to follow all their instructions—to listen to the broadcasts, keep a battery-powered radio and spare batteries handy and leave before it became too dangerous to do so.

She had ensured that both properties – Mandy's house and her cottage – were as well prepared as they could be. There were fire breaks around each one, and sprinklers too. The large water tanks were full after a wet winter, but the rain meant there was growth everywhere which had dried into fuel.

Hannie checked the backup generators every three months, because the sprinklers wouldn't work if the power was cut off, which sometimes happened on days of extreme fire risk. There were no second chances if things got hairy.

Despite all of that, living in the hills meant she was constantly on edge; adrenalin was always flowing on high fire danger days. She had to be ready to make the snap decision about whether to stay or whether to go. It was not only physically exhausting but emotionally draining, too. And Hannie had two people to think about now—one of whom had increasingly limited mobility.

Speaking of Mandy, it was almost time to take up her lunch. Hannie stocked her cane carry basket with the quiche and salad she'd had in the fridge, and added a bowl of fruit salad.

Working on her own meant she had a lot of time to herself, so it was never a chore to walk up the gravel road and across the main lawn to the house to have lunch with Mandy. As she walked over, Hannie thought about why Mandy had invited her to stay in the cottage. Had she known eighteen months ago that something was wrong? Had Mandy decided back then that she needed someone around to care for her if she got worse? Was Hannie her insurance policy for living up here at Reynolds Ridge on her own?

Hannie blinked away the image of the "For Lease" sign in the shop window next to the Organic Café on the main road.

She couldn't think about that now.

And she couldn't think about Dylan Knight, either.

Chapter Five

JUST AS HANNIE was taking the warmed quiche out of the oven, a car pulled up outside, its tyres loud on the gravel of the driveway which snaked up from the main road and curved in front of the back door to Mandy's house.

Hannie popped her head up and peered out the kitchen window. Her heart sank. It was Alice, in her late model fancy schmancy gleaming clean car, which looked like it had just been washed by a team of young men at a car wash. Alice fixed her hair in her rearview mirror before stepping out, as if she was on her way to a job interview, not a visit to her mother.

She was immaculately put together, as always. A sleeveless white linen shirt knotted at her waist topped navy linen shorts and a pair of wedge heels completed her chic look.

Hannie looked down at her outfit. Cut off denims, a bright pink tank top and Indian leather sandals. She was never going to be glamorous. She had never been vain or concerned enough to make sure she looked just right whenever she stepped out of the house. She made ornaments for a living – but she had no desire to be one herself. And, any-way, there was simply no competing with Alice – Hannie had learnt that a long time ago – so she should stop being envious of her. She tried to ignore the flicker of it in the back of her mind.

Hannie slipped the quiche onto a large platter and tucked a knife beside it. She gathered three plates instead of two and three glasses for the table.

The back door opened and a hot breeze followed Alice inside. It ruffled her straight bob and Alice quickly tucked it back into place.

"Oh, Hannie. Hi." Alice looked her up and down.

"Hi, Alice. You're just in time for lunch. Ham and cheese quiche."

Alice came over to the kitchen bench and stared at the dish as if it were road kill. "Oh, no. I'm vegan. I don't eat eggs. Or dairy."

"Oh. Well. There's a Greek salad, but"—Hannie paused—"I'm sorry. I've already put feta cheese in it."

Alice shook her head. "No, thank you."

Hannie sighed as she took the third plate and put it back in the cupboard. Just another thing for Alice to be cross at Hannie about.

"Where's my mother?"

"She's in the living room, reading. I was just going to take this in to her."

"Wait a minute on that, will you? I've been anxious to

have the chance to talk to you. Alone."

Hannie sighed. "Can it wait until after lunch, Alice? The quiche is still warm."

"It can't actually. I'm going to talk to Mum – again – about finding her a new place to live. It's just not safe up her for her anymore. She's not as young as she used to be, and that fall the other day scared the pants off me. God, Hannie, what if she breaks a hip next time and she's lying out there for hours and then there's a fire? I mean, she was all alone."

For fourteen years, Alice had found new and imaginative ways to stick the knife into Hannie's back. "You don't have to worry. You know I work from home. I'm here most of the time."

Alice crossed her arms and frowned. "You clearly weren't the other day when she needed you."

Hannie gritted her teeth. "I was with a client on the other side of the city. I wasn't far away."

"But you've admitted it yourself. You were away, which means you're not here all the time, are you? She needs to be somewhere where there is care around the clock. With staff to help her if she has another fall."

Did Alice know? "Are you saying you want to put her in aged care or something?"

"I've been discussing it with Simon and we both think it's for the best. This property is valuable. If she sold it, there would be enough to cover all the entrance fees and ongoing costs and she'd have some left over."

Plenty left over, and she knew exactly who would want to get their hands on it. She looked at Alice, tried to be impartial about what she was saying. Of course Alice loved her mother and, in part, Hannie couldn't argue with the concern about the fall and her age. With her own suspicions growing, she had thought herself that it would be safer for Mandy to move.

But it couldn't happen like this, not with Alice telling her mother what she should do. Mandy was tough and independent-minded and if she was told, rather than convinced, she would rail like a bull at a gate and refuse. Hannie's advantage was that she knew Mandy as both an aunt and a friend, a friendship she cherished and respected. Alice only knew Mandy as her mother.

However, at the end of the day, Hannie wasn't Mandy's daughter. Alice was. She tried to approach the issue diplomatically. "By what you've said, it doesn't sound like your discussed this with your mother."

"No. Not yet."

Hannie shook her head. "We both know what she's like, Alice."

Alice lifted her chin haughtily. "I know she'll listen to you. You'll have to speak to her about it. She seems to disregard everything I say and every idea I have."

"Perhaps it's the way you say it," Hannie replied.

Alice's reply was quick and icy cold. "What do you mean by that?"

"Not everything has to start out with an accusation. Alice. If you listened more, you might hear the truth."

Hannie knew how Alice worked. Fourteen years ago, the day after the school party, Alice had come over to Hannie's house. When Hannie had answered the door, Alice had screamed in her face. "This is all your fault. You've been trying to get Dylan all along, haven't you? You're the reason I broke up with him. He cheated on me with you. I'll never forgive you, Hannie, you bitch."

Hannie slipped two folded serviettes on the tray. Why were those memories so vivid, still? She cleared her throat. "Have you tried talking to your mother?"

"You know she won't talk to me about this stuff."

"Well, try harder. If you come in here acting like a matron, she's going to get her back up." Hannie loaded up a wooden tray with the quiche, the salad, and the plates and took them into the living room.

Mandy put her book down on her lap as they approached. Her injured ankle was propped up on a pillow on the long sofa.

"Hello, darling," she said to Alice who'd walked in behind Hannie. "What are you doing here?"

"Thought I'd come up and see how you are." Alice sat in one of the two armchairs opposite the sofa and leaned forward, her elbows on her knees, her fingers entwined together. "How's your ankle? Are you in any pain?"

"Oh, nothing really. It throbs a bit. I've had much

worse."

Hannie was a silent witness to the conversation between mother and daughter. She sliced the quiche and added a scoop of salad to Mandy's plate before handing it to her.

"Thanks, Hannie. You're a treasure."

Hannie didn't miss the sharp look that crossed Alice's face.

"Mum, Simon and I have been talking…"

Mandy was about to put a piece of quiche into her mouth. She stopped. It dangled in midair.

"Yes?"

Hannie sat on the other armchair, across from Alice, watching as the tension twisted her lips.

"Your fall… we're worried about you. We think it's time for you to move."

Typical Alice. She'd obviously learnt nothing.

Mandy chewed a piece of quiche. She forked up a tomato with a chunk of feta and ate that, slowly. Then, she plastered a smile on her face and said, "Nope."

"Mum," Alice implored. "At least listen to what I have to say."

"You can talk all you like, darling, but I'm not going anywhere. I'm perfectly fine here in the home I've lived in for fifty years. This is the house I came to the day I married your father, you know. Eighteen years old, I was, and madly in love. Every inch of this house contains a memory of him. I'm not leaving it."

Alice flicked a glance at Hannie, looked for moral support. Hannie sat back in her chair.

"But Mum, it's not safe for you anymore."

"It's perfectly safe. And Hannie is a minute away and she does a pretty damn good job of making sure I'm fine. I'll never go hungry as long as she's around. If I need anything, I can call her."

Alice gave Hannie a sideways glance. "Yes, well. Which brings me to my other point. Simon and I believe you should be charging a proper rent for the cottage. It's not fair to you that she pays nothing but a peppercorn rental for something that could bring you in hundreds of dollars a week. All that foregone rent could be in the bank earning you extra income. It could help you pay for the care you'll need."

Mandy's cutlery clattered on her plate. Hannie startled at the sound.

She slowly turned to face her daughter. "Stop right there."

"But, Mum, she—"

"Not another word. It was my decision to ask Hannie to live in the cottage and it's still my decision. Honestly, Alice. What on god's earth led you to believe that that was any of your damn business?"

"I'm your daughter. That gives me the right."

"No, as a matter of fact, it doesn't. Is there anything else about my life you have an opinion about?"

Alice said nothing. Her lips were pinched together in a

snarl.

Mandy smiled at her daughter. "Good. I'm glad we got that out of the way. Now tell me. How are my grandchildren?"

LATER THAT AFTERNOON, Hannie was back in her workshop. Her iPod was playing and her favourite songs filled the silence as she began to work on Beck's piece. She'd spent a lot of time that afternoon, once Alice had left, thinking about mothers and daughters and the legacy one left the other. Beck wanted to create something for her new baby, Bella, an heirloom which had memories of her own grandmother, to create memories for the next generation. No matter how much some railed against that love and that concern, mothers and daughters were linked by more than simply DNA. Despite their disagreements, she knew that deep down Mandy loved her daughter and she knew Alice loved her mother.

She hated to admit it, but she could see Alice's point of view on one thing. Her cousin might not have had the best style of approaching it, but part of her argument was right, that Mandy should consider moving. And she wasn't even aware of Mandy's health issues.

The trouble for Hannie was that there was a subtext to what Alice had said. She'd basically accused Hannie of ripping off her aunt, of exploiting her generosity by staying at the cottage. If Alice only knew that she had bigger plans for her life and her business.

But how could she move ahead with them now, with things so uncertain with Mandy's health and the potential that she was only going to get worse. Dylan had mentioned Parkinson's Disease.

That night, after Dylan had left, Hannie had hit her laptop to consult Dr. Google. She hadn't known anything about the disease, what the symptoms were or what the prognosis was.

But she knew all of that now. If it was Parkinson's, it was only going to get worse. Sure, there seemed to be medications available to lessen the symptoms, but there was no recovery.

Hannie wondered if she should tell Alice about Dylan's suspicions. But that would involve going behind Mandy's back, betraying her trust and all the love she had shown her by allowing her to live in her cottage.

Once again, Hannie felt stuck in the middle.

At school, it had been between Alice and Dylan.

And now, it was between Alice and Mandy.

Chapter Six

HANNIE WAS ON a roll.

The disagreement between Mandy and Alice two days before, and all the thoughts in her head about her future, had inspired her in a way she couldn't control. She had risen early on both days and, despite the continuing heat, had been at her desk sketching and thinking and working the metal of the heirloom piece Beck had given her. From experience, she knew that when inspiration struck, it was best to forget everything else and work. While Ted protested as he usually did when he wasn't getting his run outside, he was happy enough to sleep by her feet in her studio while she worked.

Hannie loved the quiet of her cottage and her studio. When the fire risk was low, she loved the calm serenity of Reynolds Ridge. Aside from her visits to Mandy and letting Ted outside for a pitstop, she had been at her desk all day and in the evenings, too. She was so happy about the piece she was crafting for Beck. Hannie had decided on a brooch in silver. She'd formed three hearts out of the metal and fitted them to their points met, almost in a circle shape. At the point of meeting, she'd set three of the small diamonds from the vintage piece, and there it was. The three hearts – representing grandmother, daughter, and granddaughter – were strongest when they were joined, and the diamonds shone and sparkled where they met.

Hannie had just finished soldering the brooch clip to the back of the circle of hearts when Ted growled and sat up. When she checked, his gaze was fixed on the hallway.

She never locked her door out here, no one did. There were footsteps on the slate tile and Dylan appeared in the doorway to her studio.

Ted barked in a greeting and Hannie tugged off her glasses and blinked.

"Those things are weird," Dylan said with a chuckle.

When her vision cleared she saw he was holding a bottle of bubbles. There were drizzles of condensation on the dark green bottle.

"What's that for?" she asked.

"I thought you might like a drink."

She shook her head, as if waking herself from a daze. "What time is it?"

Dylan glanced at his watch. She did too, noticing his strong, tanned forearm. "It's four."

She shook her head. "No thanks. I don't drink when I'm working."

He stepped into the room. "Why? Is it dangerous or

something?"

"I work with sharp tools. What do you think?" She reached for a tiny pair of pliers and squeezed them in his direction.

"Then I think you should probably put down those tools and have a drink with me."

Hannie cocked her head. "What makes you think I want a drink with you?"

"Put it this way. I want a drink and I thought you might like to join me."

Hannie tried to read his expression. He wasn't giving much away. The bubbles did look cold, which would mean they would also be delicious. And they were neighbours now, right? There wasn't a law that said she couldn't have a drink with her neighbour. Perhaps this was what they needed to make sure they were on the same page with everything.

"I'd love one." Hannie hopped of her stool and Dylan followed her to the kitchen. "I'll be back in a minute. I need to wash my hands. The flutes are in the cupboard above the toaster."

Hannie made a quick beeline for the bathroom. She splashed cool water on her hands and squirted some rosemary and orange hand wash into her palms. It was her favourite. Then she flicked her face with cool water from the tap and wiped her hands on a towel. She'd been sitting at a desk for almost two days straight and she needed that. She checked her reflection in the mirror above the hand basin.

Her face was bare of makeup, her cheeks were flushed from the heat. She hoped it was from the heat. Her black hair was piled on top of her head in a messy bun. And it would do. She was who she was. She didn't make a habit of waiting around the house fully made up in case a man came calling. She snorted. Who was she all of a sudden – Scarlett O'Hara?

When she returned to the kitchen, Dylan had already popped the cork and had poured two flutes full of honey-coloured liquid.

"Here," he said as he lifted one to her.

"Thank you." She sipped the cold bubbles and savoured the pop and sweetness against her tongue. It really was delicious. She sighed with delight.

Hannie wondered if she should wait for Dylan to break the silence. He'd always seemed the strong, silent type to her back in the day. But there was something about the look on his face that said *unsettled*. He was frowning and his eyebrows were knitted together. He'd said before he needed a drink. Had something happened?

She decided *she* wasn't the strong, silent type. She could be a friend to him, right? A shoulder to cry on, so to speak? "So, Dylan. What's got your knickers in a twist?"

Dylan almost spurted his champagne across the island bench at her. "What?"

"Well, you turn up on my doorstep saying you need a drink so I figure something must be up."

He grinned. "I lied. That needing a drink thing? That

wasn't the exact truth."

"What is the truth then?"

"What I should have said was that I wanted a drink with you."

Damn the tingling that started in her toes and shimmied up her legs.

"I thought you deserved it. I've seen for myself how much you've been helping Mandy. Preparing meals for her. Hanging out her washing. Feeding her chooks and collecting the eggs. Chasing after that damn goat."

"Zelda."

"The goat's called Zelda?"

"Yep."

"After Zelda Fitzgerald?"

"Yes." Hannie almost swallowed her tongue. Dylan, the football dude, the butch firefighter, knew who Zelda Fitzgerald was?

"Don't look at me like I'm a dumbass. I know who Zelda Fitzgerald is. We studied *The Great Gatsby* in high school, remember?"

"YEAH, OF COURSE."

He continued. "So, I've seen you running that whipper snipper all day and all the damn night to make sure the grass around her house and yours is kept low."

She looked him and waited a moment to process all that

he'd just said. "You mean to tell me that you've been sitting up on that veranda of yours and spying on me?"

He shrugged his shoulders and grinned. "I'm up there on the ridge. It's the perfect position to spot grass fires."

That look on his face was doing all kinds of things to Hannie. Things she couldn't admit to. "That is bullshit, Knight."

"It's true. You know how bad the weather's been the past few days. When that north wind gusts, and the temperatures are as high as they've been, anything could happen. The whole region's on severe bushfire alert."

"I know what a fire danger day looks like, Knight. I grew up here, just like you did, remember?"

"I know, I know. Give me a break, will you? It comes with the job. Professional firefighter by day. Volunteer firefighter every hour I'm not on the trucks."

"Did you know the police have been patrolling the ridge again?" Hannie took another sip of bubbles. "I've seen the patrol cars around the place. On the back roads." The boys and girls in blue made a habit of it in the summer, when known firebugs cruised the hills, lighting devastating fires and watching them destroy property and livestock and livelihoods and, tragically, people. In recent years they'd even taken to knocking on their doors, letting the suspected arsonists know they were being watched. Hannie couldn't imagine what kind of thrill a fire gave someone. Those people needed help; that was for damn sure.

"Who do you think I've been working with?" Dylan said quietly.

"Oh. The police? Really?"

He nodded. "This is a secluded spot, especially with all the small tracks here in the valley and up to the ridge. Someone could get up to no good and no one would ever see. So when I'm off shift, I keep a lookout."

Hannie decided it was reassuring to have someone so close to keep an eye on people and properties. Very reassuring indeed.

"Well, that's good to know." She raised her glass to him in a salute. "Cheers to you, our regular neighbourhood fire warden."

"Cheers to you, our regular neighbourhood good samaritan."

Hannie was taken aback at his description of her. She didn't think of herself that way. She often felt guilty that she didn't do as much in the Reynolds Ridge community as she would like. The netball club always needed coaches and umpires. She'd played all through her school years, not very well but with incredible team spirit, but hadn't gone near the club in years. Then there was the local library and the tourist information centre and the community garden. They all needed people but she'd been reluctant to get involved. She told herself it was because she was getting her business up and running and what with seeing clients, designing and making the jewellery, her promotion and publicity, and social media work, she had little time left over. She'd been doing more and more around the property as well, to keep Aunt Mandy safe. And there were only so many hours in a day.

Dylan picked up the bottle and topped up their glasses. "So, Hannie. Tell me about you. Your life these days. What you've been up to." He pulled up one of the barstools at the kitchen bench and sat down. He was settling in for a chat. Hannie sat down too.

"What's there to know? You know me. We've known each other since we were kids. We caught the same bus to school every day for twelve years."

"A lot's happened since those days," he said. "It's been a long time since we've seen each other."

Oh, the tingles. At the sexy sound of those words on his lips, there were sparks in her stomach and behind her breastbone.

And then, Justin Timberlake.

Hannie heard the song in her head as if it were blaring from her iPod.

It was "Cry Me a River". It had been playing when he'd kissed her.

She hadn't been able to listen to that song in all the years since.

She glanced down at the pattern on the kitchen bench. Rubbed her finger over an imaginary stain. "Yes, it's been a long time. Fourteen years."

He leaned forward, his elbows on the bench, his eyes focussed on hers. "So, tell me, Hannie. Are you a swinging single or what?"

She swallowed hard and the bubbles of her champagne almost snorted out of her nose. "What?"

"You seem to live up here on your own. I haven't seen anyone else coming or going."

"Binoculars again?"

"I've been looking for arsonists, remember? It's my job to take note of any unfamiliar registration plates."

"You won't be seeing any unfamiliar registration plates around here."

"Oh?" Dylan's eyebrows lifted.

Hannie went for diversion. "What about you? Did you leave a trail of broken hearts all over Melbourne then?"

As well as in Reynolds Ridge?

"Just one."

"The poor woman."

He looked up quickly. "It wasn't a woman. It was me."

Hannie didn't know what else to say in response to his honesty. They'd never had an adult discussion before, come to think of it, which made her realise she didn't really know him at all. She knew what he looked like, and was very aware of how he'd improved with age and experience, but she had no idea about what was inside that impressive package. Who was he now?

"Is that why you came home?"

"It was time," he said. "Mum and Dad needed to sell and I decided at about the exact same time that I'd been away too long. I missed the hills, the quiet. The cherries in summer and the apples in winter. The local wine and the restaurants." He studied her face. "My brother let me know about a job back here in the fire service, so my timing was all right." He hesitated. "For a change."

There was something serious in his face she couldn't read.

"How is Caleb?"

"He's good. Working in the fire service."

"Same as you then?"

He thought on that. "Yeah. It must be the twin thing."

"Is he married? Does he have a girlfriend or anything?"

"I reckon there's something going on with someone, and I'm sure he'll tell me all about it when I beat it out of him."

Hannie smiled at the memory of how the Knight brothers were with each other. Competitive, teasing, loving. It was something she'd never had, being an only child. She'd hoped to have had it with Alice, but they'd been too different as children and now, as adults, there was no trust or respect.

"Hey, tell me something?" Dylan nodded in her direction.

"What?"

"How come you never left?"

Hannie lifted her chin. "I did leave."

"That's right. After your mum sold up."

"I shared a house for eighteen months with some people I used to work with at the bank."

Dylan almost choked on his champagne. "You worked in a bank?"

"Yes. Why is that so shocking?"

He regarded her, studied her eyes. "You, the high school kid with the multicoloured hair and the books and the clothes and the attitude?"

"What attitude?"

"You know what I mean. You always walked around school thinking you were the smartest girl around."

Hannie couldn't breathe. "I did not!"

"Yes, you did." He laughed at the memory. "All that time in the library and all those books you read, like you were ticking them off some giant list so you could get into university or something. And us football players? You thought we were just a bunch of stupid jocks. You never hid it either."

If only he knew how good she'd been at hiding things. Still was.

"I never thought you were a stupid jock. And even if I did, you've just proven me wrong by knowing who Zelda Fitzgerald was."

He laughed out loud, and it hit her like a shot of whiskey down her throat.

"And you know what? You've proven me wrong, too. You're not what I was expecting, that's all. But come to think of it, I don't know what I was thought you'd be doing now. I figured I'd find you working in a hipster café or an alternative record store or something."

"What's a record?"

She loved his smile. So much. And she loved teasing him. "They're making a comeback you know. When I bought my folks place I inherited an old player and all their records. If you like Neil Diamond and Peter Frampton, you're in luck."

"Can't say I'm a huge fan of either of them. But no, no cafes or record stores for me. I had to find a real job. I don't know if you remember that Mum and I were on our own."

He was quick to interrupt. "I remember."

"She was working all the hours she could as a casual teacher and, anyway, jobs in hipster cafés don't pay the rent. Some of those owners tend to have a hipster attitude when it comes to wages, as well. You know, like we should all be paid in fresh air and quinoa."

Dylan burst into warm laughter and the sound of it was as sweet as the popping of the bubbles in her champagne.

"I never remember you being this funny," he finally said.

The air left her lungs. "Well. Surprise surprise."

"So, go on. After the share house, you came back?"

Hannie nodded. "I was starting my business and Mandy offered me the cottage. I found it hard to say no. There's something about Reynolds Ridge that keeps pulling you back."

"I get that."

"I just… never felt settled down there on the plains. This is what I know. This place is home. Being here, I'm still close to where I grew up. I won't be staying at Mandy's forever, but this will do for now. Here, at the cottage, the whole valley still seems like mine. Everything I've ever wanted is here. Except for the snakes and bushfires. And the occasional screams of mating koalas."

Dylan laughed at the memory. "Can't say I've missed the sound of that up in the trees. Hardly sounds consensual, does it?"

"I bet those girl koalas don't even get a glass of champagne first or anything."

His eyes darted to hers.

Oh shit. What the hell had she just said? Hannie felt like someone had applied a blow torch to her cheeks.

"I bet they don't. A real man knows that there are certain steps he should follow if he's interested in a woman."

"There's a playbook?"

"Oh, definitely. There's a certain etiquette a man has to follow when it comes to dating. First"—he held up his glass—"champagne."

Hannie tilted the glass and emptied it.

"And then, dinner."

"You're kidding."

"Not kidding. So, how about it?"

Dylan and Hannie held a gaze. Something was buzzing between them and both knew it. Hannie couldn't say yes to dinner with him. She'd spent years living with the guilt of breaking her cousin's heart. And he didn't have great form either. He'd cheated on Alice. With her. They'd both been complicit in her pain and anguish.

Wouldn't spending time with Dylan take her right back to all that?

Before Hannie could open her lips to say no, they heard her name being called. Their heads turned at the same time in the direction of the front door. Both recognised who it was.

Alice.

"Hannie? Where are you?"

"Back here in the kitchen." Hannie pressed a hand to her right cheek. Here she was, drinking champagne with a man – Dylan, no less – looking pink-cheeked, talking about koala sex and dinner. What the hell would Alice think?

And why the hell should Hannie still care? Alice had moved on. She was married with two delightful children. She'd found someone to give her everything she wanted in life.

Yet. Hannie still felt the hot licks of guilt at her insides.

There were clickety-clack footsteps on the stone hallway floor and then Alice appeared. She shot Hannie a frustrated look before registering that she wasn't alone. And when turned her attention to Dylan, her lips parted on a word and she stopped the admonition which she'd clearly been planning to deliver.

"Dylan Knight?" Her expression transformed from frustrated to – what was it – triumph?

"Hey, Alice."

"Oh, my god. Dylan!" Alice tottered towards him and threw her arms open wide.

He didn't get up from his stool and her petite stature meant she was at the exact same height to plant a whacking great kiss on his mouth. On his lips, Hannie noticed. She then threw her arms around him and clung to him like she was a seagull and he was a hot chip.

"How are you, Alice?"

"It's so good to see you, Dylan." It was a moment before Alice released him from her grip. She stepped back, flicked a glance at Hannie, something which looked like red hot anger, and propped her hands on her hips. "What's this all about?"

"We're drinking champagne," Dylan said, glancing at Hannie.

"Are you back to visit your folks or something?"

"No, I'm back for good actually. I've bought my family's place up on top of Reynolds Ridge."

"Really?" Now she turned to glare at her cousin accusingly. "Hannie hadn't told me any of that news. Well, welcome home. I must get your number. You and your wife should come over for dinner with Simon and me and the girls. Come and see the house. And the pool and the tennis court. It would be so great to catch up."

"He's not—" Hannie started to correct Alice on the question of Dylan's marital status, but stopped herself mid-sentence. That was Dylan's business not hers. She couldn't get in the way of this reunion.

Suddenly, all those tingles she'd been feeling in her toes and everywhere else turned into icicles. In a blink, she was right back where she had been a million years ago, in her school uniform, with her school bag laden with books on her shoulders, watching Dylan and Alice in love.

If the champagne bottle wasn't already empty she would have snatched it from the table, lifted it to her lips and sculled whatever was left.

"Life's good then?" Dylan asked.

Hannie tried to judge, on a scale of one to ten, how happy he appeared to be to see Alice.

It was a five.

"Life's fantastic, actually." And then as Alice began to witter on about Simon's career and her lovely house and her lovely kids – all of which was objectively true – Hannie faded out.

She picked up the empty bottle and the empty glasses and took them to the sink. She stopped a moment to catch her breath, peering out the window, checking out the late afternoon sky.

Which is when she saw the smoke over the top of Reynolds Ridge.

Chapter Seven

"DYLAN."

Alice continued to talk, as if Hannie hadn't said a word.

"Dylan." Hannie spun around from the window. There was a pounding in her chest now for a whole other reason.

He was looking right at her. "What is it?"

"There's smoke over the ridge."

Alice stopped mid-sentence.

Dylan leapt up from the stool at the kitchen bench and rushed across the room in four big strides to Hannie's side. He dropped his head down to check out the view through the low window.

"Damn it." He straightened, fished in the pocket of his shorts and pulled out his phone, jabbing the screen and pressed it to his ear. Something beeped. He reached for the pager tucked into his waist band. While they were thought of as old-fashioned technology to some, the devices were still the backbone of a fire response in parts of Australia as mobile phones could lose range, especially in parts of the winding

Adelaide Hills.

Dylan looked at Hannie a long moment, then he turned. "It was good to see you, Alice. I've got to go and deal with this."

He strode towards the hallway and was gone. A moment later, they listened as his car drove off in a loud roar.

"How close is it, do you think?" Alice rushed to the window and to Hannie's side.

"It's hard to tell. I'm not sure which way the wind is blowing."

They exchanged glances. All the animosity Hannie had felt in the air disappeared. Times like these meant petty disagreements were put aside. There was an immediate understanding between them, borne from years of living in the hills during summers.

"I'll pack her bag," Alice said.

"I'll help you," Hannie replied. The cousins ran up to the main house and in ten minutes, they'd packed up Mandy's papers and valuables – always safely stored in a suitcase during bushfire season – and Mandy was buckled up in the passenger seat of Alice's car.

She wound down the car window and leaned out to talk to her niece. She wore the kind of frustrated scowl Hannie knew too well. "I would be perfectly fine staying here. This is all such a silly overreaction. I've lived through worse fires in these hills and you know it."

"Not with a sprained ankle, you haven't." Hannie tried

to find some cheer in her tone so Alice wouldn't get a clue as to what she was really worried about. "And stop your complaining. Think of it as a little holiday. You'll be better off with Alice down in the city until we know what's going on. I can hold the fort here; check the tanks and the pumps and the irrigation on the roof. Don't worry about Zelda and the girls. Dylan will keep me informed about what's happening. Don't worry. Everything will be all right." Hannie reached down to clasp her aunt's shoulder. She gave it a little squeeze.

Mandy looked up at her. There were tears welling in her aunt's eyes. And then it hit Hannie like a scorching north wind. Mandy knew her limitations now. This was a show for Alice, to put on an act in front of her own daughter, to be strong when all she was feeling was fear.

Hannie leaned close, kissed her aunt's cheek. "Everything will be all right," she whispered.

Then, out loud so Alice could hear, she said, "Stop being so difficult. Let that daughter of yours pamper you and make sure you get the grandkids to read to you, this time."

Alice looked over the roof of the car, a quick glance before she slipped in to the driver's seat.

Thanks, she mouthed silently, grimly.

"You right, Mum?"

"Let's go," Mandy said, winding up her window.

Hannie stood in the driveway until the car had driven all the way down the gravel drive to the main road. Then she raced back down the hill to her cottage, burst through the front door and flicked on the radio positioned on the bench top next to the fridge. She was always tuned into the Australian Broadcasting Corporation, the official emergency broadcaster in times of disaster. At times like this, it was a welcome relief to hear the calm tones of the announcer Hannie recognised from last summer.

"Winds are turning east to north-easterly throughout the afternoon with an increased bushfire danger rating from severe to extreme. There are very hot, dry, and windy conditions expected. If a fire starts and takes hold, it will be extremely difficult to contain and will take significant resources to bring it under control. Spot fires will start well ahead of the main fire and cause rapid spread of the fire. Embers will come from many directions. The safest place to be is away from bushfire prone areas."

Hannie's heart pounded in her chest and, despite the champagne she'd shared with Dylan, she was wide awake and alert, the adrenalin coursing through her. According to the radio and the information from the emergency services, the fire was about ten kilometres away and fast approaching the small township of Normanton, about twenty kilometres north east of Reynolds Ridge. The advice to residents there was to leave now.

Nothing about Reynolds Ridge yet.

There were things to do to secure her property and Mandy's and, for an hour, she checked pumps and the generator in the main shed. If power lines were down, which often happened when high winds felled trees, there would be no mains power, so people in the hills had their own generators for their irrigation systems, to spray their houses with water if fire approached. She really didn't have to do all this checking; it was part of her weekly routine during the bushfire season, but it calmed her to double and triple check. During her work, she could see the smoke rising higher and higher in the sky and, worryingly, it wasn't just white now. There were dark puffs too, and she knew what that meant. It wasn't just trees that were burning.

Dark, almost black, billowing smoke in the distance meant that buildings had been lost—sheds or homes or businesses. She quickly went back inside to her radio. With a long glass of iced water, she sat in the kitchen, fidgeting, hanging on every word of the emergency broadcaster for any news, for any change in conditions, for any new warnings. Reynolds Ridge was southwest of the fire at Normanton and the wind was blowing from the south. She hoped that meant it was blowing away from the ridge, but nothing could be reliably predicted in a bushfire. Embers could travel kilometres and land in long grass, sparking new fires. Wind could change direction in a moment, and flare dying flames. Lightning strikes could set up fires anywhere.

She was aware, ready to go if she had to. She made sure Ted was securely tied to the leg of the table in the kitchen, so she had one less thing to worry about. She looked down at his face and worried for him. Ted was like a radar system for her. He knew when someone was in the house. He seemed to sniff a change in the wind. And when the weather was like this, he never left her side.

"You're a legend, Ted, you know that?" Ted's eyes squinted in delight as she scratched him behind the ear.

As she listened to the radio, she absent-mindedly stroked his back. She took in every detail of the advice from the Country Fire Service and the police about evacuations and warnings.

They continually reminded people. "Stay until it's not safe to do so. If you are planning to leave, leave early in case your escape route is compromised by smoke of fire, or fallen trees or loose power lines."

She was taking in so much information, listening so intently to the radio, Hannie hadn't realised it was dark outside until she looked through the kitchen window to check on the dark smoke and saw the night.

She picked up her phone and called Mandy.

It picked up after one ring. "Hannie? Are you okay?"

Hannie breathed deeply to hide any panic that her aunt might read into what she said. "All good here. Just thought I'd let you know that we're still standing."

"We've been watching it on the news. It sounds like the wind's blowing in the right way for us. Did you see that three houses have been lost in Normanton?"

"It's awful, isn't it?"

"I hope it's not the Porters. They've got that plant nursery there off the main road."

"Me too." But Hannie knew that if it wasn't the Porters who had lost their home and potentially their livelihood, it would be someone else, possible someone else they knew. Fires were indiscriminate, random, and devastating.

"Now, Hannie, listen up." Mandy's voice lowered conspiratorially. "That daughter of mine is being a right pain in the patootie. She's insisting I should stay down here tonight."

Hannie breathed a sigh of relief. "She's right. Why don't you stay put there? I'm sure Natasha and Ainslie will adore having you for the night. I'll let the chooks out in the morning if things have settled down and check on Zelda."

Mandy's voice seemed suddenly fragile. "You don't mind?"

"Of course I don't mind."

"Okay then. Perhaps I will. Have you heard anything from Dylan?"

Hannie hadn't. She knew plenty of the men and women from around the ridge who jumped on the Country Fire Service trucks as volunteers when bushfires hit. Half her high school class, in fact. Everyone was on edge, waiting for them to return home safe. But this concern about Dylan was different. It had crept in to the space behind her chest, and was growing bigger as the day had worn on.

"No, I haven't. I'm sure he's fine. He knows what he's

doing."

And, reassuringly, there had been nothing on the news about any injuries – or worse.

"He hasn't called you?"

"No. I don't even think he has my number."

Mandy chuckled. "Why ever not? You stay safe, Hannie. Natasha has just brought me a pile of her favourite books that she's insisted her nanna should read to her. Oh, look here. *Possum Magic*. I'll see you tomorrow, Hannie."

"See you tomorrow."

Hannie ended the call. She tucked her phone in her pocket and went to the heavy wooden back door, opened it, and then pushed the screen door open. The air smelt faintly of burning fuel and eucalypts. It was eerily quiet all around the property. The wind seemed to have settled down too, which would help stop the fire and embers from spreading. Hannie lifted her eyes up to the top of Reynolds Ridge. There were lights on at Dylan's house.

She didn't think twice. She raced back inside and grabbed her car keys.

HANNIE HAD BARELY stepped foot out of her four-wheel drive when she heard Dylan's voice.

"Hey," he called. He was standing on the veranda, which ran along the back of his long, rectangular stone house. The lights from inside glowed and she could just make out the surprised smile on his dirty face. He was still wearing his protective yellow trousers and his fire boots, but had stripped off his helmet, jacket, and T-shirt.

"Hey," Hannie said. She clutched her keys and her phone in one hand and walked towards him. She willed her eyes not to fall below his chin.

"This is a surprise." He stepped off the veranda and walked towards her, slowly.

He was standing there and he was okay, looking at her with a bemused expression on his dirt-smudged face.

Hannie wanted to lift her hands to her throat and wring her own neck. What the hell was she doing? Why had she jumped into her car and raced up the ridge on an unlit, dirt back track in almost the middle of the night to see if he was okay? And why were her hands shaking?

"Well... I..." She could hardly admit she'd been scared shitless all day worrying about him, could she? "Do you know anything about what was lost in Normanton?" she blurted out.

That bemused expression on his face became sombre. He ran a hand through his messy blonde hair. "Two homes. Some storage sheds."

"Oh, damn." Hannie gasped, covering her mouth with a hand in shock. "And the Porter's nursery?"

"Their home was saved but the business is gone. The shade-clothed nurseries and everything that was in them."

"That's awful news."

Dylan came closer. "But the Porters are safe, Hannie. They listened to the warnings and did what they had to do. They left in time. No one was hurt. No lives were lost."

Hannie closed her eyes against the memories in her head, which came flooding back. Her mother's grief at losing her husband. The long, long months and the tragedy of it, so fast, so sudden, the inexplicable agony of never saying goodbye, the pervasive dread of imagining the flames and the fear. And then the grief and the rage was reignited months later when the coroner's findings were handed down, revealing he'd died from a heart attack trying to flee the fire. There was little relief in knowing that he'd already been dead when his car had been incinerated.

A strong hand on her shoulder pushed those memories deep down. There was a new sensation—warm fingers against bare skin. A strength calming her. When she opened her eyes, Dylan was close, looking down at her.

He cocked his head back to the house. "Since you've come all this way, you want to come in for a drink?"

Hannie felt dizzy. She was tired and hungry. In her nervous anticipation of what the bushfire was doing throughout the afternoon, she'd actually forgotten to eat. Without thinking, she brought a hand to her stomach.

"Or maybe something to eat?"

His hand was still on her shoulder, reassuring, gentle. He was so close to her she could smell the smoke in his hair and the sweat from his labours.

"I haven't had dinner," she murmured as she looked up at him.

He took his hand away. "Although the volunteers of the Country Women's Association supplied the most amazing sandwiches today, I'm hungry for something more substantial. Feel like a steak?"

She sighed and smiled back at him. "Yeah. I'd love one."

When he reached for her hand and tugged her forward, she let him.

DYLAN OPENED THE back door and stood aside to let her in first. Hannie stepped right in the kitchen. She'd never been inside the Knight's home when she was younger so she took it all in for the first time. It was a big old country style kitchen, with Baltic cupboards all around the walls and a long farmhouse table in the centre of the room. There was a new stainless steel fridge on one wall and on the bench, a coffee machine, a toaster, a microwave, and a food processor. It was neat and tidy. And there were ripe, purple plums in a white bowl in the middle of the table.

The door closed behind her and Dylan gently urged her forwards.

"Why don't you grab yourself a drink? I really need to take a shower and get out of this gear. There's wine and beer in the fridge and… you know the drill."

With a quick smile, Dylan strode off down the hallway

and a few moments later, she could hear the sound of a shower running. She opened the fridge and saw two steaks marinating in a dish, an unopened bottle of wine in the door, and enough vegetables to make a decent salad. She took out some cherry tomatoes, a bag of rocket, a cucumber, a jar of semi-dried tomatoes and some marinated feta. There was a loaf of bread in a paper bag on the bench next to the fridge and she sliced a few pieces. She opened every door until she found the dinner plates and inspected every drawer until she found the cutlery.

Five minutes later, when Dylan emerged freshly scrubbed, hair towel-dried but still damp, wearing a singlet top and some loose shorts, she had already made the salad, set plates out on the long table, and downed half a glass of a delicious Adelaide Hills sauvignon blanc.

He stood open-mouthed in the doorway. "What's all this?"

"I'm starving. I thought I'd get things going while you were cleaning yourself up."

He strode towards her, reached into the salad bowl for a square of feta and tossed it into his mouth. "Remind me to invite you around for dinner more often," he grinned.

"Tell me something, Knight. Do you always have two steaks marinating in the fridge in case of a drop-in?"

"They were both for me, but I'll share with you."

Hannie popped a cherry tomato into her mouth. "That's very generous of you."

Dylan rubbed his hands together. "Now where are those steaks?"

"ANOTHER WINE?" DYLAN held the bottle up so it was hovering over Hannie's glass.

She quickly covered it with a flat hand. "No, I should go. It's late." She looked up to the big carriage clock over the door to the hallway. "It's eleven thirty."

How had three hours passed so quickly? A delicious steak, cooked medium-rare to perfection, a green salad, fresh bread, and a crisp wine had enticed her to stay longer than she thought she would.

They'd just spent a few hours getting to know each as adults, navigating around what they thought they knew about each other and what they didn't know about each other's families and filling in some of the gaps. And totally ignoring what had happened between them fourteen years before.

Dylan was funny. He was thoughtful. His eyes shone when he laughed and when he looked at her… oh, the tingles.

Major league tingles.

Hannie reached for her keys and phone and stood up. His chair scraped back too.

"Thanks for the steak. And the wine," she said.

"It was nothing. Especially since you helped."

Hannie went to the back door but Dylan made it there first and opened it for her.

"We should do this again, sometime," he said as they walked to her car, their footsteps crunching on the gravel drive.

Another sometime with Dylan was not a good idea. Ever. She didn't answer but left his offer hanging in the warm night air.

She reached the car and turned, her keys in her hand, gripping tight. That's when he stepped close and she automatically took a step back until her ass hit the car door. He reached a hand out and touched the lock of hair that had come loose from her rough bun. His face grew serious as he twined her hair around an index finger.

"Your hair used to be short," he murmured.

"Yes."

"And all kind of crazy colours."

"Sometimes."

The night around them was pitch black and quiet. There was a rustling in the tall gum trees by the shed on the other side of the driveway. Possums, she supposed.

He didn't let go of her hair. Then his other hand was on her arm, stroking slowly from her wrist to her elbow. He wrapped his fingers there, and his touch was so soft she wanted to sigh into it, to close her eyes and linger on the feel of it.

"Hannie." His voice was a murmur in the quiet. "I never asked you. Is that short for something?"

"No," she whispered. "It's just Hannie."

His face was close to hers. His mouth was a moment away. The tingling in her toes turned into a flash of light which shook her whole body awake. To stop herself losing her balance she lifted her hands and splayed them on his chest. His breathing caught and then there was a long, slow exhale. Under the fabric of his T-shirt she felt hard muscle and bone. They were so close to each other her wrists were pressed backwards up against her breasts.

"Just... Hannie," he said. And as he said her name, low and deep, he leaned down and touched his lips to hers.

Lightning struck her. Dylan Knight tasted like wine and the cool night air. Kissing him felt so right she fell into it as easily as breathing. She moved her hands higher until they met at the back of his neck and she pulled him in closer, arched herself against him, so the kiss was deeper, suddenly more urgent, faster, bolder. She felt the kiss in every cell in her body. She melted and burst into flame all at once.

They came up for air, gasping, then his lips were on her cheek and then lower, to the place behind her ear where her hair tangled; and she lifted her head to the stars and he kissed down her neck to her shoulder. He pushed himself into her, god, already hard, and then a hand was on her left breast, cupping her, his thumb flicking over her nipple which had tightened in a primal siren song for his lips.

And then she heard Justin Timberlake in her head, crying about a river.

She pulled away. Tried to find her breath. She looked up

at him in the dark. His eyes were wide, his lips open. He rubbed a hand over his hair.

"Fuck," he said, as if he'd suddenly woken from a dream.

"Dylan …" She remembered who she was and what she'd done. Her last mistake had cost her in ways she still regretted. "This was …" she fought for breath, for sense. "God, this was so stupid."

His shoulders stiffened. "You think I'm stupid?"

"No, no. It's me. I'm the stupid one. We can't do this. Not again."

He held out a hand for her, but she slid sideways along the car and out of his reach. "What do you mean, not again? Hannie? What are you talking about?"

She turned to him and pointed angrily, her finger wagging in the space between them. "You, me, and Alice. Don't tell me you've forgotten?"

His eyes flashed and his jaw clenched hard. Then he took two big strides to her, brought his hands to her arms. "I've never forgotten that."

"Then you must know what we did to Alice. Remember?"

His brows knitted together. "I don't know what the fuck you're talking about. All I remember is what you did to me."

Hannie felt hot now, dizzy. "What?" She tugged herself free. "I've really got to go. Ted will be waiting to be let out."

His words were almost lost in the dark. "Yeah, you're right, after all. This was fucking stupid."

Chapter Eight

OVERNIGHT, THE WIND had settled into a gentle breeze but, at daybreak, it heaved and throbbed and was now a blistering northerly, sweeping up all the heat from the deserts of central Australia and blowing thousands of kilometres south to scorch and parch the whole of South Australia.

At Reynolds Ridge, the wind tore leaves from the plum trees in the valley below and the heat that came with the fierce wind shrivelled orchards full of fruit just as they were ripening in the valley. When the sun came up they had been plump and red. A couple of hours later, they had split and burst, been tossed to the ground, ruined.

Hannie hadn't slept. She'd tossed and turned, sweat and sleeplessness combining to make her bleary-eyed and groggy as the sun came up. She stumbled out of bed and went straight to the fridge for a cold glass of water. Ted whimpered in his bed in the corner of the kitchen, a spot he preferred because it was the coolest part of the house, so she undid his leash and opened her back door. He tried to bolt outside but Hannie pulled him back. It would only be quick pitstop and then she'd take him back inside where it was safe and cool.

The wind hit the back of her throat, parching it. There was something familiar and frightening about the heat. In the sky, the clouds were moving so fast they looked as if they were running from something; great white puffs stretched and bloomed and grew. Hannie sniffed the air. It smelt of crisp, dry heat but, thank goodness, no smoke.

But the wind. It was like a monster come to life. The trees all over the property were bending into shapes she'd never seen; clawing sideways as if they were begging with outstretched hands. She knew what winds like this meant. When fierce winds hit, the limbs of trees became flying weapons as they flew into overhead power lines, ripping them from their poles and dragging them to the ground.

With that came further risk of fires and blackouts, too.

Southern Australian summers really were unforgiving and cruel.

There was nothing Hannie could do but wait. She walked Ted to the grassed area at the side of her cottage and waited while Ted sniffed around before doing what dogs had to do. He made it quick. He didn't like this wind either. As she turned to head back inside the house, there was the unmistakable sound of a car turning into the gravel driveway from the main road. When it approached, she recognised it as Dylan's.

He pulled up and was walking towards her before she

could even think about what had happened the night before. That stupid, reckless kiss. Their second stupid, reckless kiss. One that had kept her awake all night, tossing and turning and thinking about the man she couldn't have.

He strode towards her, his face grim.

"Hello," she replied, trying not to come over all *I-wasn't-up-all-night-thinking-about-you-no-shut-up-it was-the-wind*. Ted leapt forward, tugging in the lead, trying to reach Dylan. *Get things back to neighbourly*. She scolded herself. Pretend last night never happened. Pretend it ended with a goodbye at his door and a wave goodbye, not a kiss and his hand on her breast and his need pressing into her belly.

"I'm about to head to the station. Everything okay here?" He strode over, looked her over, his Adam's apple bobbing up and down at this throat.

She looked down. Oh. She'd walked outside wearing the clothes she'd slept in. Her knickers and a thin singlet top.

"That wind is bad," she said, looking up in to the sky. That was safer territory. The weather. The sky. The heat and the risk. Not the kiss. Not the way he'd been looking at her just now.

"North-north easterlies. You've heard the forecast."

She nodded. He didn't have to ask her, he knew that she would be prepared every day in the bushfire season. That was what came with the beauty and serenity of living in the Adelaide Hills. Green and lush in winter, but in summer, it was part of the driest state in the driest continent on earth.

"Mandy's staying down in town until the cool change arrives," Hannie said, hoping to sound businesslike. "At Alice's." She looked across the valley. There was no sign of that cool change arriving any time soon.

"Good to hear. She'll be safer down in the city until her ankle heals. I wouldn't want to see her trying to evacuate with that injury."

"I don't think that'll be an issue. Alice probably won't ever let her come back."

Dylan cocked his. "What?"

"Oh, nothing." She averted her eyes from his inquisitive gaze.

Hannie shook her head. She couldn't tell Dylan the truth about his first love, could she? That Hannie feared there was some big plan in place to force Mandy to sell the property?

"The kids will love having their grandmother there, that's all."

"Right." Dylan took a step closer. "You going to be all right up here on your own?"

A prickle of anger rose in her. "You think I don't know what I'm doing?"

He frowned at her, settled his feet apart in a wide stance and crossed his arms over his chest. "I am the professional firefighter. In case you hadn't noticed."

She had noticed. From his daffodil coloured helmet in his hand to his protective yellow jacket and trousers, he was every inch the expert. She looked Dylan up and down, from the top of his buzz-cut hair to the steel cap of his boots, stopping for just a fraction of a second on what was in between. Strength. Heat. Muscle.

All forbidden to her.

It wasn't that blasting north wind that was frying her brain. It was Dylan Knight and the memory of that damn kiss.

"You know I've lived here all my life."

"Yes."

"And you know that I know what I'm doing." She'd evacuated more times than she could count with her mum, their four-wheel drive packed to its roof with their secured plastic containers filled with all the important papers in the house – insurance papers, wills, passports – and their precious pets. Charlie the lab when she was a child, then Oscar the next lab when she was a teen.

Dylan was close now. Almost as close as he'd been the night before when he'd pressed his lips to hers and scorched her.

"So stop bossing me around. I've lived through bushfires, Knight. I've taken all the steps recommended by your colleagues in the Country Fire Service. Look around. There's no tall grass here. I've checked the generators and my water tanks are full. I have a battery-powered radio and enough food and water to last a week if we have power blackouts. I've cleaned leaves out of all the gutters on Mandy's house and my cottage and the lawns are mowed. And, yes, I have an evacuation plan in case you're wondering."

She shouldn't have to convince Mr Macho-Firefighter-Teen-Crush that she knew about bushfires. But she felt the need to show off. Just a little.

He shook his head. "Why did I even think I had to ask?"

"Because you're you, that's why."

He studied her face for a moment and she wished she could see behind his reflective sunglasses.

His mouth remained a flat line. "Don't take any risks, Hannie."

"I won't." She'd learnt from bitter experience that taking risks hurt and that the consequences could be lifelong.

Despite what had happened last night, she didn't want him to worry about her staying at Reynolds Ridge when he was supposed to be at the station or on the trucks, saving people and property.

He turned to go, and then looked back. "Because, even though I would do it in a heartbeat, I'd hate to have to get all official on your ass."

"You're not getting anything on my ass, Knight."

His jaw twitched before he turned away. As he strode off, he called out, "When the fire's out, we're going to talk about last night."

"There's nothing more to say," she shouted after him.

Dylan stopped. Turned. "Oh, yes there fucking is."

Then he got in his car and drove off to fight the fires.

Chapter Nine

I T WAS THE best sound in the world. The *plop-plop-plop* of raindrops on the tin roof of her cottage. When she heard it, Hannie lifted her eyes to the ceiling and breathed a sigh of relief so deep it emptied her lungs.

The weather forecasters had been predicting it would rain, that the cool change would sweep up from the south-west to blanket the city and the hills with rain, and it had finally arrived.

"Hear that, Ted? It's raining. Your favourite thing. If you're really lucky and we get a decent downpour, there'll even be water in the creek in the gully. I might take you down there for a swim, hey?"

Ted sat up and whimpered in excitement. She undid his leash and threw open the back door and they stood together in the rain. Hannie let it soak through her T-shirt and her shorts, her hair and closed her eyes and turned her face to it, drinking it up in joy.

It had been a long day and a long wait for the rain to come, but at nine at night, it had delivered. The forecast was for ten millimetres, a decent soaking for the Adelaide Hills, which would extinguish all the embers that had been blowing around from the Normanton blaze, and settle any smaller grass fires that could have potentially flared. In the morning, the State Emergency Service crews could continue their work clearing tree branches from roads all over the hills, and people could perhaps return to normality for a while.

Until the forecast turned again.

Hannie took Ted back inside and tethered him in his bed. She poured herself a long glass of water and gulped it down.

When the fire's out, we're going to talk about last night.

Dylan's words had been going around and around in her head since she'd heard the rain. What was she going to do? It didn't feel safe to be around him but how could she tell him that? She'd have to lie. She'd have to pretend that kiss was a big nothing and she wasn't interested in him in that way.

"We should just be neighbours." Yes, that was what she should open with.

And it was true. For months now, she'd been working on plans to move out of the cottage on Mandy's property into a place of her own, with a shop attached if she could find such a place. She'd been grateful for Mandy's offer, as it had allowed her to really get her business up and running with low overheads, but she was doing well now. Jobs were steady and Hannie had done her sums. She had socked away money in the bank and she was almost ready to make the leap. She wanted to be out on her own, to prove to herself that she could make her dream of her own business come true.

While she was still torn about what was going on with Mandy, it would be so much better to be further away from Dylan. Knowing he was there across the valley had become unbearable. So close and yet so untouchable.

Ever since the night of the school party all those years ago, Hannie had tried to repair her relationship with Alice, to make up for her betrayal. She had hoped that staying with Mandy and looking after her aunt and the property has been part of that bridge-building, but Alice seemed to resent her for it instead of being grateful.

They had been young, hadn't they? Couldn't they be forgiven a stupid mistake?

She'd kissed her cousin's boyfriend, Alice's first love.

And worse, he'd kissed Hannie, too.

They'd broken Alice's heart and were still paying the price for it.

IT WAS TEN o'clock when Dylan drove up to the cottage.

Ted growled a moment before Hannie heard the sound of tyres on gravel. Hannie was sitting at the kitchen bench on a high stool, her fingers knotted together. The hair on the back of her neck prickled when she heard the footsteps outside and then the knock.

She'd known he'd keep his word. He was that kind of

man.

"Come in," she called.

Dylan walked through the unlocked door and strode into the kitchen. He wasn't wearing his fire fighting uniform, but jeans and a worn T-shirt. His hair was wet and pushed back and Hannie smelled soap.

"You shouldn't have bothered coming over," she said. "I don't think there's anything more to say."

"I don't agree. We're finally going to talk about what happened."

She spun on her chair and stared at him. "You mean what happened all those years ago?"

"And last night."

Hannie gritted her teeth. "We kissed each other. We shouldn't have. That's it. It can't happen again. End of story." She swivelled her chair away from him.

Dylan walked to the kitchen bench, stood opposite her. Hannie focussed her attention on the fruit bowl between them. It was full of plums and she stared at them to distract herself from his penetrating gaze.

"You wanted me to kiss you."

The plums were plump and purple. The stems and leaves were bright green and fresh. "So what if I did?"

"You liked it."

"Yes, I did." Hannie squeezed her eyes shut. She'd more than liked it. She'd been hungering for it ever since.

"And you kissed me back."

She let out the breath she'd been holding. "So what if I did?"

She heard his long strides on the slate floor and then felt him close. His hands were on her shoulders and he swivelled her around on the bar stool. Her clamped-together knees pressed into his strong thighs.

"Hannie," he said, "I want to kiss you again."

"No, you don't," she replied, in barely a whisper.

"Oh, yeah, I do. And then I want more. I want to fuck you right here on the kitchen bench."

"Oh, god." She gasped and he put his hands on her knees and stroked up the bare skin of her thighs, into the legs of her shorts.

She spread her knees wide and Dylan moved in, pressed himself closer, up against her. Tingles became an explosion. One of his hands moved from her thigh to her neck, splaying against the skin under her ear. She kept her eyes closed and shivered at the feel of his warm breath on her cheek.

"You didn't want me when we were in high school. Do you want me now?"

She pulled back. "What did you just say?"

His eyes were dark as the night outside. "Fuck, Hannie. Don't make me say it again. You kissed me that one time, all those years ago, and then nothing. You dumped me. I was crazy about you, didn't you know?"

Hannie's head spun. She planted her hands on his chest to keep his lips away from hers, so she could get her thoughts straight. "You were crazy about me?"

"For months."

Hannie's eyes stung. "I wanted you, Dylan, but you weren't mine to want. You were with Alice. That night we kissed, when I would have given you everything, you were hers. I wanted something I could never have and I took a stupid risk and betrayed my cousin. Wanting you now makes me feel exactly the way I felt back then. I can't betray her again."

The fingers on her thigh gripped hard. "I wasn't with Alice when we kissed. We'd already broken up. On the night of the district Grand Final."

That had been in late September. Reynolds Ridge High had thumped the Normanton High boys by ten goals. She'd been watching the whole game with Alice at the school oval. Dylan had kicked six of those goals. Alice had told her she was going to give him her virginity that night, to celebrate. The school party had been a week later, just before school ended for the year.

Hannie felt sick. "No… no… no."

Dylan ran a frustrated hand through his hair. His other hand was still on her thigh. She looked down at it, his tanned fingers against her pale skin.

"Look," he said, "I know I was an eighteen year old kid full of hormones, but there's no way in hell I would have kissed you if I was with someone else. No fucking way."

Hannie tried to breath. "But she screamed at me that

night at the school party."

"She was angry and jealous. I tried talking to her but she stormed off."

"But the next day, you weren't there. She stood on my doorstep and screamed at me some more. She accused me of trying to steal her boyfriend."

"She did what?"

Hannie's head throbbed.

She could either believe Dylan or Alice. And she knew, in that moment, that she couldn't choose her cousin, not after how she'd been treating her all these years, like the poor step-sister in some crazed fairy tale, letting her hang on a lie all this time. For fourteen years she'd made her feel guilty.

But this wasn't a fairy tale. This was real life.

"All these years …" Hannie finally managed to say. "She's been lying to me all these years."

She looked up. Dylan was gazing down at her.

"You thought I'd cheated on Alice."

Hannie nodded.

"That's why you didn't talk to me after that."

She nodded again, her heart pounding in her chest, her palms sweating, her head light and spinning.

"And she kept the lie up to keep us apart, didn't she?" Hannie said quietly. "Out of some kind of twisted revenge or something."

"It sure as hell looks like it."

Hannie reached for his T-shirt, gripped her fingers in the

fabric and pulled him in close. She took a deep breath and slammed her mouth to his. And all the heat of the scorching Adelaide summer was in that kiss.

Chapter Ten

HANNIE MOVED FAST. There were so many pent up years of longing in her heart that she didn't want to waste a single second.

She pulled Dylan's T-shirt off over his head and pressed her lips to his chest, all tight muscle and bone and naked skin that tasted like soap and man and sex. She felt his breath catch in his throat when she licked his pec and bit his nipple, and she looked up at him, saw his dark eyes blazing, watching her, and she trailed her tongue up his chest, along his neck and jaw to his bottom lip and she found his mouth and kissed him again. She slipped her arms around his neck and pulled him close and somehow his hands found the hem of her singlet top and got it over her head. Then, with a quick flick, he'd unfastened the clasp of her bra and that was off, too.

"Fuck, Hannie…" He moaned when he took in her bare breasts and then he dropped his head to one nipple, sucking it and nipping it with his teeth, and then the other, and it was so good and she was building and building and the tingle became a throb.

"I want you." She groaned.

He chuckled deeply against her lips. "You got me."

And then he kissed her again and her whole body responded to his mouth by throbbing, aching, demanding release and needing him inside her.

"Dylan," she said, pulling away so she could speak. "Condom. Now. The bathroom."

He gripped his arms around her and lifted her off the stool. She wrapped her legs around him, pressing herself against his stomach, wanting the pressure of his body against hers, and as he strode down the hallway, she kissed him again, rubbed against him, splayed her hands in his hair.

She stopped only just long enough to open the medicine cabinet on the wall and grab a box of condoms she kept there.

He grinned. "Think that'll be enough?"

"Surprise me, Knight."

When they reached Hannie's bedroom, he sat on the edge of the bed and Hannie pushed him backwards until his back hit the sheets. She slipped off him to tug down her shorts and her knickers and he kicked off his shoes and jeans and then she climbed back on him and, as soon as he'd ripped the foil wrapper open and protected himself, Hannie found him with a hand and moved over him and he thrust up and filled her and she closed her eyes and felt every inch of him inside her.

His hands were on her hips, tight, and she arched herself back and rode him and splayed her hands on his chest and then fell forward, knowing this was how she would come too, and when she did, she bit her lip and held her breath, and then he came, with a thrust that felt like she was riding a bucking bull. He slowed, closed his eyes, and they tried to catch their breath and slow their pounding hearts and they looked at each other, in disbelief, in shock, in total lust.

"Hannie," he said.

She slid off him and dropped to the bed by his side, boneless, sated, in a daze.

"Uh-huh," she replied.

Dylan got off the bed, went down the hall to the bathroom and came back. She propped herself up on her elbows to watch him. He really was magnificent naked. Tall and lean, and with the kind of muscle definition one get from exercise and hard work, not hours in a gym staring at themselves in the mirror. But it was his smile that got her right in the solar plexus. Oh, his smile. He slowly climbed over her and covered her with his body. She spread her legs to let him settle against her and he kissed her, gently, softly, slowly. Her lips tingled. She was sure they would be swollen tomorrow. She didn't care.

The light of the night sky left the room in semidarkness. He was more than a shadow; his eyes were bright and his smile the same.

And when she felt him hard, pressing against her, she

lifted her head. He wanted her again?

"Really?" she asked.

He moved against her, hard and hot and huge, as he kissed her and when she lifted her hips, he said with a sexy grin, "You wanted me to surprise you, Reynolds."

"I did say that, yeah," she said, feeling brain-fuzzed.

"Surprise," he said in her ear as he pushed himself against her again.

She fought the urge to spread her legs and take him in and, instead, fumbled on the sheets for the box of condoms. Dylan moved backwards off the bed and stood before her, watching as she tore the foil.

"You want to do that for me?" he asked.

Hannie looked at him, took in every muscle, every plane of his body, and shook her head.

"Not yet." She edged forward.

His cock was almost up against his taught belly and she suddenly didn't want to cover it with anything but her hands and her mouth. Hannie moved closer to him, dropping her legs over the edge of the bed, squeezing his calves between her knees, and she took him in her hand, wrapping her fingers around him, tight, then loose then tight, sliding her palm the length of his shaft, listening to his breathing deepen, watching his chest rise and fall.

"You're incredible," she whispered and when she pressed her lips to his cock, kissed him, and then ran her tongue along the silky skin, he gripped her shoulders and moaned her name.

She opened her mouth wide and took him in. His legs shook and his hands moved to her head and he tangled his hands in her hair, like handcuffs around his wrists. He pulsed against her tongue and then he pulled out, reached for the foil package by her leg and rolled the condom on in half a second flat.

She moved backwards into the middle of the bed and he was on top of her, kissing her mouth, her cheeks, her nose, and saying her name in a whisper and a moan and then he was inside her again, and she moved in a rhythm with him, as instinctive as it was unspoken, and they came together on a cry that filled the room.

DYLAN BROUGHT A glass of water to her bedside.

"Thanks," she said as she gulped it down. "Hot sex and a cool drink. The whole package."

Dylan laughed. "It'll take more than water to cool you down, Reynolds." He kissed her again and pressed her deeper into the pillow.

"What can I say? You lit a fire in me, Knight." She laughed. "And I seriously now can't think of any more fire clichés."

"Listen." He sat by her on the bed, stroked the hair from her cheek. "I'm on call and I need to be home with all my gear."

"I understand," Hannie said.

He searched her face, distracted. "You have beautiful hair, you know."

"Thanks."

"It's like running water through my fingers." He twisted a curl around a finger. "You want to do something tomorrow? If my pager doesn't go off, I mean?"

"Sure. That would be great."

"Why don't I come by at ten and pick you up. Wear your bathers and bring a towel."

A swim sounded amazing after all the hot weather. "Sure."

She lifted her head up and kissed him and he kissed her back with every bit of the longing she'd put into it.

"See you tomorrow," he said.

"Yeah."

Hannie watched Dylan pull on his jeans and his shoes, wrangle his T-shirt over his head. His smile didn't dim the whole time.

The last thing she remembered before her eyes fluttered shut in satisfied exhaustion was him pulling the sheet up to cover her, and one more warm kiss on her lips.

DYLAN WAS TRUE to his word.

At ten, he pulled up in Hannie's driveway.

She was waiting for him at the back door, wearing a sundress with her bathers underneath, sandals, and a sun hat. She had a beach bag slung over her shoulder filled with a bottle of water, a plastic bowl for Ted, and a big tube of sunscreen.

"Hey," he said. He walked to her, slowly, grinning like an idiot.

"Yep." She grinned right back at him.

He slipped an arm around her and pulled her in close, kissing her as he smiled against her lips.

When Ted whimpered at her side, Dylan reached down and gave him a scratch behind the ear. The dog plopped himself down on his butt and his tongue lolled to the side.

"You want to bring Ted to the beach?"

"Would that be okay? It's just that with his knee surgery, he hasn't had the chance to run around, and I figured he'd love having a splash in the waves."

Dylan reached for the beach bag slung over her shoulder. He hooked a couple of fingers under the strap and lifted it off. "Absolutely no problem. He'll have to sit in between us in the middle. He doesn't get car sick or anything, does he?"

"No. He'll just dribble on us."

Dylan shrugged. "I've been dribbled on before, mostly by people who've had too much to drink."

They walked towards the car, Ted straining on the leash with excitement. Hannie kind of knew how he felt. She was going to spend the whole day with Dylan.

"So which beach are we going to? Glenelg? Grange?"

Hannie asked. He opened the passenger side door and lifted Ted into the seat.

"Port Elliot. I thought we could have a swim at Horseshoe Bay. Sound good?"

Hannie sighed. "That sounds like heaven."

Chapter Eleven

HANNIE WASN'T SURE who loved the beach more—her or Ted. It was no secret that Labradors loved the water, but his usual swim in the muddy creek at the bottom of the valley was nothing compared with the Southern Ocean and the protected harbour of Horseshoe Bay on South Australia's Fleurieu Peninsula.

It had taken them an hour to get to the idyllic place, south from Reynolds Ridge along the South Eastern Freeway to Strathalbyn and then on to the pretty coastal spot. It was a summer haven for holidaymakers from the city and the hills and, today, the calm beach of Horseshoe Bay was the perfect spot for everyone who'd sweltered through the past week of blasting summer temperatures. There were children dragging body boards into the water, toddlers paddling in the shallows wearing life vests for safety, and striped beach canvases fluttering in the wind, straining their pegs which had been pushed into the sand.

Hannie and Dylan had feasted on some fish and chips for lunch, then washed the meal down with a chocolate malt milkshake, and had finally given in to Ted's desire to get in to the water. He still wasn't supposed to run, so Hannie made sure he was firmly attached to his lead.

"Here," Dylan said, adjusting his straw hat, "I'll take him. Why don't you go have a dip?"

"You sure?"

"Absolutely."

Hannie but her lip. "We could maybe try to tether him to something so he doesn't run off."

Both looked down at Ted who was standing to attention, his tail horizontal, staring straight ahead at the waves crashing on to the sand.

"I don't think that's going to work." Dylan said. "I get the idea that if he had the chance he'd head into that water and swim all the way to Kangaroo Island."

Hannie laughed. "Yeah. You're right. I won't be long."

Dylan dropped to the sand and stretched his legs out in front of him. He looked mighty relaxed in his board shorts and loose T-shirt, which was nice to see. She'd become used to seeing him in his regulation yellow fire fighting outfit, steel-capped boots and helmet and everything. He needed this too, perhaps more than she did.

Hannie lifted her sun dress over her head and dropped it on the sand. She flicked her sandals on top of it so it didn't blow away.

Yeah, he looked. He dropped his head and did a long, slow journey up her body, along the curve of her calves to her thighs, past her rounded hips, her breasts barely constrained in her one piece that plunged down at the front.

She turned and sauntered to the water. When she waves began splashing her hips, she dived in.

DAMN TED.

The hound hadn't actually done anything wrong except be his big, loveable slobbery self.

Dylan was stuck on the sand, minding the dog, when what he really wanted to do was be out there in the water with Hannie, with his mouth on hers and his hands all over her body.

He was gone. One night and he was done. Tasting her, fucking her, being in her bed, that was what home felt like, he'd realised as he'd driven from her place to his the night before.

So many wasted years, so much water under the bridge. All because of Alice's drama queen games and bullshit. She had driven him away from Hannie once before, but there was no way in hell that was going to happen again.

"Whoa, big fella." Ted had startled and when Dylan looked up Hannie was walking back up the beach, slicking her hair back from her forehead, looking like a freaking sun tan lotion commercial. Man, she was beautiful.

Her smile, her sass, her ass. Yeah, he liked her ass. He liked everything about her. Even with his dog-minding duties, this was turning out to be a pretty great day.

As he watched her walk up the sand from the waves, his thoughts drifted back to the toast his cousin Logan had recently made at their grandfather's wake. "To getting laid and fighting fires."

Dylan thought he should change that toast. "To finding the right woman and fighting fires."

That was something he would toast to any day of the damn week.

"The water is amazing," Hannie announced when she was at his feet.

She looked relaxed, her legs slightly apart, and drops of water were drizzling over every part of her body. Shimmering little droplets, sand particles shining on her legs, the curve of her hip, and in the deep V of her swimsuit where the curve of each breast swelled.

Dylan went to speak but his tongue was thick and he felt drunk all of a sudden.

Hannie in her bathing suit, with her smile, with that warm energy, had rendered him speechless.

"Here, let me take Ted. You go swim."

He stood up, handed her the leash, ripped off his T-shirt and sprinted to the water.

HANNIE SLIPPED ON her sun dress to protect herself from the warm afternoon sun, shoved Dylan's T-shirt in her beach bag, and led Ted on a gentle walk along the lapping shore-line.

Horseshoe Bay was a big curve, with a surf lifesaving club, restaurant, cafe and children's playground at one end, and a rocky outcrop at the other. She walked in the opposite direction of the crowds of people, the swimmers and the families and the body boarders, and walked along the edge of the water.

It had been a great day. From Dylan's ready acceptance of Ted's presence, slobbering in the seat between them all the way down to the beach, to lunch, to the laughs, to his dazzling smile, to the sight of him in his board shorts running into the water.

Last night had been about pure, primal need. They'd fucked like two people who couldn't be sated unless they were joined, as if they had been satisfying some long-buried, primal urge.

TODAY IT WAS about something more. Now, she could barely keep her hands off him. In the car on the way down, she'd reached over Ted and stroked Dylan's cheek, which made him grin. When they'd been sitting on the freshly-mown lawns by the cafe eating their fish and chips from a cardboard cone, she'd leaned across and kissed him, licking the salt and vinegar from his lips. Her body was giving her signals that were impossible to ignore. She wanted him in a way she hadn't wanted anyone in forever.

As she walked, splashing in the shallows, she put together a plan for that night. They were going to make a serious dent in that box of condoms. She hadn't been in a relationship in a while, but she was ever hopeful and it had sat in the bathroom cupboard for a year. She had a stash of local cheese in the fridge and some artisanal crackers in the cupboard and a bottle of Adelaide Hills sauvignon blanc chilling in the fridge. All for after they'd fucked each other senseless, of course.

Yeah, that sounded like a plan.

"I wondered where you'd got to."

She turned. Dylan. Handsome as hell Dylan Knight was right there smiling down at her. She sighed at how happy she felt, how content. This beach, Ted, and this man. A perfect day.

"I thought Ted deserved to get himself wet."

Ted barked up at them, as if he was agreeing with Hannie.

"Smart dog," Dylan said.

She stepped closer to him, and brought her free hand to his chest. She ran it over one of his pecs and then down his wet skin, across his abs. She stopped right there. He looked down and then covered her hand with his own.

"Hey, I have an idea."

He looked up, raised an eyebrow. "Yeah?"

"I thought maybe you could take me home right now

and fuck me."

He groaned as he leaned down and kissed her, fast, hard, demanding. "Hell yes."

FIVE MINUTES AFTER they'd left Horseshoe Bay, Hannie's phone rang. She reached into her beach bag and looked at the screen.

She pressed the screen to take the call. "Hey, Alice." Dylan looked at her, his mouth a tight line.

"Hannie, you've got to come. I'm in hospital with Mum." Alice's voice broke.

Fear skittered up her spine. "What's happened?" She closed her eyes, imagining the worst, imagining that Mandy's whole world was about to be broken into a million pieces.

"She's had another fall and the doctors think something's wrong. Something serious. I'm waiting here in accident and emergency and they're trying to find her a bed in the Neurology Ward."

"Which hospital?"

"Flinders Medical Centre," Alice managed.

"Stay calm, Alice. I'm on my way." Hannie did the sums quickly in her head. They were an hour south of Adelaide and the hospital was in between the beach and the city. She checked the time on the clock on Dylan's dash. "I'll be there in half an hour."

She ended the call with a gasp and she covered her

mouth in the shock of what Alice had just told her. Alice had sounded terrified.

Dylan reached out across Ted and gripped Hannie's bare shoulder. "Mandy?"

Hannie nodded. "She fell. She's really hurt herself this time. I should have said something. I should have told Alice about what I'd noticed. I should have told her what you thought it might be. Parkinson's. This is all my fault." She dropped her head in her hands and tried to fight the tears.

"We're on our way," Dylan reassured her. "We'll get there as soon as we can."

Chapter Twelve

DYLAN PULLED UP at the accident and emergency entrance at the hospital. There were two ambulances in the bay, one with its rear doors open and she saw two paramedics wheeling a patient towards the doors. She fumbled with her seatbelt and grabbed her beach bag.

"You'll take Ted home?"

He reached for her hand. "Call me when know something."

"Thanks, Knight," she said quietly, nervously, tears welling in her eyes. She didn't want to cry in front of him but she was too upset to care if he saw.

"See you, Reynolds." He managed a smile, too, but there was concern in his blue eyes and his hand lingered on hers.

She nodded, gave Ted a hug, and ran inside to find her aunt and her cousin.

"SHE'S HAVING AN MRI." Alice looked pale and worried.

Hannie had found her sitting in the waiting room of A

and E. Hannie had opened her arms to hug her cousin, and Alice had accepted the gesture. No matter what Alice had done, they were still cousins and they were both worried as hell about Mandy.

"She told me," Alice said quietly.

"About what? Hannie gasped.

"About the Parkinson's." Alice's face fell. She drew in a deep breath.

"It's Parkinson's?" Dylan had been right about Mandy.

"Don't tell me you didn't know."

"I know you won't believe me, but I didn't know. I thought… I thought something was wrong, that she seemed frail, but whenever I raised it she brushed me off, told me she was just getting old."

Alice turned on her, teary, and clutched a fist to her chest. "And you didn't think to tell me anything about these… suspicions? She is my mother, Hannie. I have a right to know what's going on with her."

Hannie pinched the bridge of her nose. "You do, but she didn't want to tell you either, clearly."

Alice slammed a fist against the arm of the plastic chair in the waiting room. "All this time I've been trying to get Mum to sell that damn property, so she could move somewhere more appropriate for someone her age, and you've known things weren't right."

"Wait a minute, I—"

Alice shook her head. "I know you, Hannie. You like to

keep secrets, don't you? You like to hide things from me."

Hannie bit the inside of her mouth. *Think about Mandy. Not about Alice's vindictive bullshit.* "Your conspiracy theories aren't going to help you with this, Alice. Mandy needs you. She's no doubt scared and frightened."

"And you need her too, don't you, Hannie? You need her to stay up there at Reynolds Ridge so you can keep your free ride. You don't want to lose your cosy little cottage in the hills, which you pay virtually nothing for. No wonder you haven't told me about her health and what you've noticed. You don't want that to end, do you?"

Hannie flinched at the searing bitterness in her cousin's tone. But she wouldn't' bite. Not now. She wouldn't fight Alice here in the hospital waiting room. Mandy had to be their priority. "She was obviously scared to tell you, Alice. Both of us. She didn't want you to worry about her. You know how independent she is."

Alice stood abruptly, pulling her handbag against herself like a shield. "I don't want you to see her. Get out of here, Hannie." She laughed but it was mocking, cruel. "Go home. *Home.* Not for much longer if I have my way." She turned on her heel and walked away.

Hannie felt shell-shocked. She stood slowly and stopped, trying to process what had just happened. An hour ago, her life seemed just about perfect.

Now, she realised what her cousin's plan had been all along. Alice had always been determined to ruin every good thing in her life—Dylan. Her business. Her home.

Oh, she would pick her time and place, and she was going to fight back.

HANNIE WANDERED OUTSIDE into the late afternoon and blinked into the fading sun. She wanted to go home.

But Dylan and Ted were on their way back up to Reynolds Ridge without her. She'd anticipated that she would be at the hospital for hours and hours, waiting with Alice, consoling her while doctors checked Mandy out. When she looked at her phone, she realised she'd been in and out in five minutes. She didn't want to call Dylan, even though he would have turned around in a blink to come back and get her. She needed to be alone with her thoughts for a while.

Dylan. Mandy. Alice. Her own business. Her future. Everything seemed up in the air. Alice would now be more determined than ever to sell the property out from under Mandy. For her aunt, it would be like losing a limb; she loved that place so much. But now that Alice knew about the diagnosis, which, even though Hannie had her suspicions, had still shocked her to her core, there seemed no other course of action.

But what did Mandy want? And how long before her wishes for her life would have to come second to getting her the best care?

Hannie walked around to the front entrance of the hospital and waited at the public bus stop. There were regular services making the journey north into the city, and she could get off near the main shopping strip of Rundle. Not that she felt like shopping.

When she was half an hour away, she texted Dylan.

"I'm on the bus. Would you be able to pick me up in the city in 30 mins? Corner of Pulteney Street and Rundle Mall by the lanterns. Sorry to ask. Thanks xx"

It took half a second for him to reply.

"I'll be there."

She tucked her phone back into her beach bag. She looked around at the other people on the bus and felt out of place in her brightly patterned sun dress and sandals. The bus ride gave her much needed time to think. When the bus stopped on Pulteney Street, she waited by the fast food joint on the corner, feeling angry and determined.

AS SOON AS Dylan had received the text message, he'd jumped into his car and headed west into the city, down the winding hills roads, covered with canopies of incongruous English oaks and elms, plane trees and gums. He didn't see any of the lush greenery on the trip down. All he could think about was Hannie.

Firstly, why the hell was she on a bus? While there was

nothing wrong with public transport, didn't she know he was here for her, waiting to help in any way he could? Didn't she know he would drop everything for her? She was beautiful and sexy and fun and she had a way of making him laugh like he hadn't laughed with a woman in a long time. Being a firefighter, he spent most of his days surrounded by guys. Sure, there were women firefighters in the service too, but the few there were worked on different shifts at different stations. So he hung out with the guys at work and his twin brother, Caleb, when he could, when they weren't working conflicting shifts or Caleb wasn't out being Caleb.

He missed the company of women. How the smelled, how they thought, how they talked, and what they talked about.

For a long time, after his relationship in Melbourne had disintegrated, he'd decided he was done with women. He'd told himself he didn't need the drama, that they were too much work, that he didn't have the energy to negotiate their moods and their demands. But that was all bullshit. He wanted all that with a woman just like every other straight man he knew. He wanted the drama and the moods and the demands and the fun and the laughter and, for fuck's sake, he wanted the sex.

Last night, he'd almost burst into flames with needing her.

Hannie today, in her bathing suit, dripping wet, all curves and heat and sand and salt?

He'd wanted her like he'd never wanted anyone else in his life.

He'd hit the city and driven up Rundle Street, past the cafes and restaurants and cinemas and fashion stores, until he reached the corner of Pulteney and he turned, pulling up in the first available spot, in front of a Thai place. Hannie walked to the car and got in. She gave him a half smile and did up her seat belt.

"Hey," he said and reached out a hand. He touched her shoulder. He wanted to hold her, comfort her, tell her everything was going to be all right with Mandy, that he would make everything okay. He couldn't, he didn't have that power but, damn, he wanted to.

He checked the rearview mirror and pulled into the traffic. He did a loop around the block and headed back east towards the hills.

"I would have come to get you, you know, at the hospital. Just ask, Hannie. Anytime. I'd do anything for you."

She put a hand on his thigh as he drove, and he liked it when she left it there.

"Thank you. I know you would have come back if I'd asked, but I needed time to think. Is Ted okay?"

"Ted's fine. When I left, he was asleep. Tell me about Mandy? Is she okay? What happened at the hospital?"

Hannie stared out her side window of his car. It was along while before she answered him.

"You were right. She has Parkinsons's. She told Alice.

And, of course, Alice blamed me, which I knew she would."

"You're fucking kidding me," Dylan said angrily.

"I'll tell you all about it later. Can we just go home?"

He covered her hand, still on this thigh, with his. "Sure." Dylan took Hannie home without another word.

WHEN THEY ARRIVED back in Reynolds Ridge, Dylan bypassed the gravel road to Hannie's place and looped around on the track up to the top of the ridge.

She looked at him.

"Ted's at my place, Hannie. I thought you'd want him with you tonight."

In that moment, Hannie felt it. Dylan understood her. He didn't assume she needed him to save her or tell her everything was going to be all right. She felt on the verge of something good and real with him.

But it would have to wait.

"Thanks, Dylan." She needed to process what had happened at the hospital. She needed to know that her Aunt Mandy was okay. And she needed to tell them all about her plans for her own future.

When they pulled up in front of the house, where Ted was secured by his long leash, she noticed that Dylan had filled a bucket of water for him and had put an old blanket on the pavers so Ted would be comfortable. Ted barked and his tale slashed from side to side like the plastic strip of a whipper snipper.

She got out of the car and walked to her dog, kneeled down, and pressed her face to his. "Haven't you had an adventure today?"

"And so have you," Dylan said.

She turned and looked up at him. "Yeah."

"If you want to talk about it, about anything. You know where I am."

She bit her lip to stop herself from crying. All she could do was nod.

He reached out a hand to her. "C'mon. I'll take you and the hound home."

THAT EVENING, HANNIE sat on her veranda with Ted at her feet, looking out over the valley. She tried to reflect on the good things about the day; how much Ted had loved the car ride and the paddle in the water. How much fun she and Dylan had had together.

She picked up her mobile, scrolled through her contacts. With tears in her eyes, Hannie called the one person she could talk to, no holds barred.

"Hello, Hannie," her mother, Lucy, said when she picked up the call. "How are you? Staying safe, I hope."

It was so good to hear her mother's voice. It had been so hard to say goodbye to her when she'd decided to move to Cairns, but Hannie understood. And they talked weekly –

sooner than that if they needed to – but it wasn't the same as having her close. Perhaps that was why Hannie had grown so close to Mandy.

"It's cooler today, Mum, and we're all good here. Ted says hello."

At the mention of his name, Ted's tale thumped on the ground.

"Give him a hug from me. How's that leg of his?"

"Better," Hannie said. "He's still not allowed to run around but we took him to the beach today, down to Port Elliot, and he absolutely loved it. He's exhausted now. He's lying here at my feet, asleep, aren't you, Ted?" Ted opened one eye and closed it again.

Lucy didn't answer right away. "We? Who's we?"

"Me and Ted and Dylan." She paused. "Dylan Knight."

"That name is familiar. Oh, wait a minute. It isn't that the Dylan who Alice was mad for in high school, is it?"

Hannie sighed. "The same." She'd been feeling rather mad for him herself lately.

"I remember she cried for a week when he left for Melbourne all those years ago. Your Aunt Mandy thought she was being ridiculous. Does Alice know he's back in town?"

"Yep. They ran into each other here, actually."

"Oh, I would have loved to be a fly on the wall. How is your cousin? Is she still being her usual authoritarian self?"

And that was when Hannie burst into tears and told her mother everything. About Mandy's diagnosis. About Dylan, and Alice's lies, all those years ago and her accusations today. Ted must have understood the distress in her voice, because he got to his feet and plopped his head in her lap, looking up at her with a loving expression on his adorable Labrador face.

"Damn that girl," her mother said, exasperated. "I know she's a relative, but she's a piece of work, she is. She takes after your father's side of the family." Hannie's and Alice's fathers were brothers – Mandy and Hannie's mother were sisters-in-law. "They were stubborn men, the Reynolds brothers. Always thought they were right, as if no one else ever had a thought with any merit. And that's terrible news about Mandy." Her mother paused. "You know, I'm putting two and two together and coming up with six, but I wonder if that's why Mandy offered you the cottage eighteen months ago. Because she knew already and that you'd be there in case anything happened."

Hannie wiped her eyes with the back of her hand. "I've been thinking that too. But I can't stay here forever, can I? The business is growing and I've been working on plans to move."

"Did you ever chase up that place on the main road next to the café? The one you told me about when you called last week?"

"No. I... I've been a little distracted."

"It sounds perfect for you, Hannie. Of course, it would be even more perfect if you were up here opening a business in Cairns."

Hannie managed a chuckle. She loved that her mother had never given up trying to persuade her to move to Queensland. "My heart's here in Reynolds Ridge, Mum."

"Do you want me to call Alice and give her a piece of my mind?"

Hannie startled. "Oh, god no, Mum. I can handle her. I have to give myself some time to calm down, though. If I saw her now I might just kick her in the shins. Or worse."

"Let me know how it goes, will you?"

"I will, Mum."

"Now, tell me all about what's going on with you and that Dylan Knight."

Hannie had to smile at that. It was a nice change to want to smile about something. "Something might be going on."

"Oh, darling. I'm so happy for you. That sounds nice."

"Yes, it could be." Maybe.

"Can you send me a photo? What does he look like now?"

Hannie laughed. "You want a photo? What makes you think I have a photo of him?"

"Please." Hannie's mother laughed. "You young people are always on your phones. I bet you've posted it to Instagram already." Lucy knew she had an account, but it was for jewellery only, not hot men she'd had sex with.

"I actually do have a photo." Earlier that day, which already felt like a week ago, she'd snapped him when they'd been eating their fish and chips on the lawns of Horseshoe

Bay They were both cross-legged, facing each other, enjoying the sunshine and the cool sea breeze, with Ted plonked between them. He was absolutely still, waiting for either of them to cave in and feed him a hot chip.

Dylan had broken first, and when Ted had gobbled up the morsel, he'd leaned over and licked his benefactor on the face. Dylan had burst into laughter and thrown himself back on the grass, which was the clue for Ted to leap on him and keep licking. Hannie had acted fast. She'd grabbed her phone from her bag and snuck a shot.

And just now she remembered that she'd forgotten to look at it. She hadn't needed to look at a photo of Dylan when he was right there in front of her.

"I'll send it to you," Hannie said.

"Uh oh, you've got that dreamy sound in your voice. You really like him, huh?"

"He's a great guy, Mum."

"Are you seeing him again?"

"I hope so."

"What do you mean you hope so? You don't think he'll call you or something? Hannie Reynolds. Don't tell me you're waiting around for some guy to ring you. You go and get him if you want him."

She did want him. "Thanks for the pep talk, Mum."

"Sometimes, Hannie, I wish I was closer. I still feel guilty about moving so far away."

"Oh, god, Mum, don't be. We talk all the time. And I'm

coming up at the end of April, remember?"

"And I'm counting the days, my darling girl. Now, you call me if that horrid Alice says anything else to you. I won't hesitate to call Mandy and tell her the truth about her daughter, although I have an inkling she already knows."

"Love you, Mum," Hannie said, her voice wobbly.

"Love you, too."

Hannie stared at her mobile phone for a long while after she'd ended the call to her mother. Absentmindedly, she clicked on the photo icon and found the photo of Dylan. There he was—laughing, happy, squinting his eyes, and pulling his lips together to avoid being tongue-kissed by Ted. She smiled as she sent it to her mother.

A moment later, her mother sent back a heart emoji.

My heart's here in Reynolds Ridge, Mum.

Dylan.

She wanted him. What was more, she needed him.

She patted Ted on her way through the kitchen, reached for her keys which were on the kitchen table, and raced outside to her car.

IT WAS ONLY a couple of minutes to Dylan's place. She turned into the dirt track which led to his place and drove through the front gate. She checked her face in her rear view mirror. She looked flushed. She was nervous and excited all at once.

"You go and get him if you want him." Her mum always did have the best advice when it came to men. The drive curved around and to her right, tall shrubs blocked her view of the house but as she rounded it, she saw a car parked out front of Dylan's place.

And then, she saw two people standing by the car.

One of them was Dylan.

And the other one was Alice.

Chapter Thirteen

DYLAN AND ALICE.

Hannie's throat closed over. She slammed her foot on the brakes out of pure instinct, not wanting to go any closer to what she was seeing, but the manoeuvre caused her tyres to skid against the gravel of the driveway and Dylan and Alice quickly looked up when they heard the noise.

She couldn't back down the road and she sure as hell couldn't move forward. So she was caught. She squinted her eyes closed and there she was, right back in high school, longing for Dylan and jealous of Alice. She dropped her head on the steering wheel and wished some kind of black hole would open up and suck her right up into the atmosphere, or down into hell – whichever – so she wouldn't have to talk to either of them.

There was a rapping on her car window. She reluctantly looked up.

It was Dylan. She powered down the window.

His expression was guarded. "You all right?"

No. I'm a total idiot. "Yeah, I…"

He looked back over his shoulder and then said quietly. "Alice is here."

"I can see that. I really should go."

"Don't." He reached for her arm. "She was just going. Come inside for a drink, will you? We need to talk." His expression was neutral, not smiling, not frowning, which was the face she imagined he would have to have when he broke bad news to people he'd pulled out or burning buildings and wrecked cars. *We need to talk. We couldn't find your pet cat.*

Weren't they the worst words in the English language? We. Need. To. Talk. What that usually meant was that one person needed to do the talking and another person needed to do the leaving. Dylan opened her car door and waited. Hannie turned off the engine and got out. She followed Dylan back to where Alice was waiting by her car. Hannie was still furious at Alice and was worried if she started, she wouldn't be able to stop. She still felt bruised, raw, from her cousin's accusations and from the way she'd effectively banned her from seeing her aunt.

"Hannie," Alice said haughtily and avoided her gaze by staring off into the distance just over Hannie's right shoulder.

"How's Mandy? What did the doctors say?"

"She has Parkinson's, remember? And she's been going downhill for a while. But, wait, I think you might know that already."

Hannie tried to steady her voice. "When you've calmed

down, we need to have a long conversation."

"About what?" Alice's eyes darted to Dylan.

Oh, she knew. She knew she'd been caught out in her lies.

"I think you know, but this isn't the time or the place. I'm sure your mother needs you."

Alice sniffed. "Well, here's one thing you should know. She doesn't need you anymore."

"Alice." Dylan spat it out like a command. "That's enough."

Hannie shot a glance at Dylan. His arms were crossed over his chest, his feet planted in a wide stance and there was something twitching in his jaw. He was angry. Furious, even.

Alice let out a sob. "That's it. I know when I'm not welcome." She stomped over to her car.

"Alice," Hannie called after her, "please tell Mandy that I hope she's okay. When can I visit her?"

"Never."

Hannie felt the rage suddenly rise up inside her. If Alice wanted to be the perfect daughter, perhaps she could start with a taste of what looking after the property and Mandy was like.

"Alice," Hannie called.

Alice turned her had back just a little.

"While you're here, perhaps you'd like to go down to your mother's place and see to the animals? The chickens will need putting in for the night and you may want to search through the gardens for any eggs they've laid. If we don't collect them, the foxes will eat them and no one wants them hanging around the house. And be sure to bolt the door on the coop or the foxes will get in there, too. Last time that happened it was like the Texas Chainsaw Massacre in there. And watch out for Zelda."

"Zelda?" Alice frowned.

Why was Hannie surprised Mandy's daughter didn't even know the name of her pet goat? The creature who kept the grass around the house low and safe. Who loved a cuddle and an apple from the orchard. Who bleated every time Hannie walked over from her cottage.

"The goat. And a word of warning. Don't turn your back on her. She likes butting people. In the butt."

Dylan made a weird sound. If Hannie wasn't mistaken, it sounded like a chuckle, which he masterfully masked with a strategically-placed cough.

Alice didn't take the bait. She stomped back to her car, slammed the door so hard it echoed in the valley and drove off with a shower of gravel flicking from her tyres.

"That... fucking... woman... I... can't... even..."

Dylan put a hand on her shoulder. "Yeah, my thoughts exactly."

Hannie spun around to look at him. "What was she doing here?"

"Spinning more of her bullshit."

"What did she say?"

"Some of her conspiracy theories wouldn't be out of place in some of the darkest places on the web." He shook his head in disbelief. "She claims you're trying to scam her family, that you're only living on Mandy's property to get cheap rent."

Hannie was speechless. She'd heard all of that before, but to say it all to Dylan now? Alice was still trying to ruin things between them.

He cocked his head at her. "And the only reason you've been caring for Mandy is because you're trying to ingratiate yourself into her good books so you can be left something in her will."

"You are freaking kidding me?" The anger rose up in her throat and almost choked her. "She actually said that?"

"That's when I told her to get the fuck out of my house."

"Really?"

Dylan took her by the shoulders and gently pulled her towards him. "Yes, really. You think I'm going to stand here and listen to her crap about you?"

Hannie's knees began to wobble.

He had her back. Between her mother and Dylan, she had people on her side, people who believed she had only ever wanted to help her aunt. Hannie looked up at the man standing in front of her, her defender. Her Knight in shining armour. When she'd been in love with him in high school, she could never have imagined the kind of man he would become. Loyal, honest, kind. Nice to dogs. The kind of man who looked at her and made parts of her tingle that hadn't felt like tingling in a long, long time.

She wiped the tears from her eyes and took a couple of steps into his personal space. She laid her palms on his chest. She wondered if they were still covered with grains of sand.

"When I pulled up today and I saw you with her, I... I thought you might still be in love with her. That she might have come here to try to win you back or something."

Dylan pulled Hannie into his arms and looked down at her with soft amusement in his blue eyes. "I was never in love with Alice."

She slipped her arms around his neck, tilted her head up, and then he was right there, pressing his lips to her. And that was all it took for her to melt into him, to let the kiss dissolve any other thought in her head about everything else that had been on her mind the past few weeks. She closed her mind off to everything else but Dylan and the rush she was feeling in every part of her.

When they paused, decided to give each other a moment to breath, he searched her eyes and smiled.

"I've got condoms."

She slid an arm down to his hand and tugged him towards the house.

TWO STEPS INTO the kitchen, Hannie was tugging at Dylan's T-shirt. When he'd helped her flip it over his head and tossed it on to the stone floor, she walked him backwards to the kitchen bench, closed in on him, pressed her body against his, and then touched her lips to his chest and ran her flicking tongue over a nipple. He tasted like salt and the beach and she closed her eyes and breathed him in.

"Hannie." He groaned and he reached his hands up to hold her cheeks.

Oh, god. A Hollywood kiss. Hannie waited, savoured the moment, the gasp of breathlessness, the anticipation of his taste, his strength, his gentleness. And then they were kissing again and he pulled her to his bedroom.

The early evening sun filtered through the window, casting a soft, blurred light over the room. There was a bed, that was all Hannie needed to know, and he gently put her down at the end of it. She fell back on to her elbows. Then he stepped back, grinned like a man who was about to get laid, kicked off his shoes, stripped off his socks and then slowly undid the zip on his shorts. They fell to the rug and he was standing before her in his boxer briefs, the kind that clung to the tops of his thighs and his arse and his hips and his cock, hard and urgent and pressed against his stomach.

"Take those off," she said. Her eyes dipped and she felt a throb low and strong at the junction of her thighs.

"Yes, ma'am." And then he was naked and her heart thudded and stopped, and she took in every inch of him, lean and long and ripped.

He took two steps to the bed. She got on to her knees

and flipped off her sun dress. His eyes drifted over her body and she thrilled at it. He kneeled on the bed and eased one strap off. He pressed his lips to her bare shoulder and she looked up at the ceiling, quivering with a moan that was on the tip of her tongue. Then his expert hands were on the other strap and he eased that off too, and pulled her one-piece down to her waist. He leaned down, cupped her breasts, and sucked in one nipple then the other, sending exquisite flickers of lightning to her toes and to the roots of her hair. She buried her fingers in his hair, short, rough, and then one arm was around her easing her down into the mattress and he'd stripped her too, and they were flesh on flesh, heat on heat, and the strength of him surrounded her, covered her, enveloped her. Her arms stretched over his strong back and she pressed her fingers into the corrugations of muscle she found there. She arched her hips into his and felt him, so hard.

"Hurry." She breathed.

"Hold your horses, Reynolds," he whispered into her ear.

He kissed a trail down the side of her neck, along her collarbone, down between her breasts, tickling his lips against her stomach and then, and then... she parted her legs wide and he buried himself there, and took her to the edge with a flick of his tongue and the exquisite pressure of his fingers. Her arms thrown back over her head, her back arched, and her hips bucking, she came under his touch and it was like a firestorm inside her, burning and exploding and,

VICTORIA PURMAN

when she could finally breathe, she felt as if all her bones had melted inside her skin.

"You good?" He laughed.

She opened her eyes and saw him grinning at her from between her knees. "I'm…" She struggled to find the word. "I'm…"

He moved up her body and kissed her, fiercely, and she opened up to him, their tongues dancing, their lips tangled, his breath was hers and she wasn't sure whose heart was beating inside her chest. He was hard against her, urging now and she reached down and grabbed his butt and pushed him against her. He pulled back.

He moved to the bedside table, which was covered by a lamp and a stack of books. He whipped open a drawer and then ripped the foil pack open with one hand and his teeth.

"Let me," she said, feeling drunk on him.

He was back on top of her, his skin hot and as soft as velvet under her fingers. "Too late, darlin'."

And with a thrust that she needed, wanted, craved, he was inside her and kissing her and she was kissing him back just as hard, a dance of two people who weren't quite sure where this passion had come from, but craved each other like a fire needs fuel.

With a groan in her ear, Dylan came and his body slowly unwound, and his mouth was at her ear, whispering. "Reynolds." He said it with a groan mixed with a sigh.

"Knight."

He lifted his face from the crook of her neck to look at her. She held her breath. His look, his soft expression, the way he stroked her cheek, was more intimate than the sex. That realisation rocked her. She moved, cradling him more closely in the swell of her hips.

"You are…" He was lost for words. He exhaled and chuckled.

"So are you," she said back.

For a long while, they lay entwined, neither wanting to move, to break this spell. There was a gentle breeze from outside, and they listened in wonder to the echoing, throaty call of magpies in the tall gums on Dylan's property.

"Isn't that a beautiful sound?" he said. "I missed that when I was living in Melbourne. I didn't realise how much until I moved back."

"Was it hard? Coming home, I mean?"

Dylan moved slightly, taking his weight from her and settling next to her, his body still pressed against hers. She relished the warmth of his skin. He trailed a finger around her belly button, which made her laugh, and then he cupped one of her breasts, leaning over to kiss her nipple with wet lips.

"If you do that again I might come on the spot," she murmured.

He grinned and took her whole nipple into his mouth, laving it with his tongue.

She laughed and pinched him.

He let go of her, kissed her breast, and looked into her eyes. "No, it wasn't hard coming home. And it won't be hard staying with you here."

She would never forget this moment with Dylan.

This perfect moment.

Chapter Fourteen

F OR THE NEXT four days, Dylan was at work at the fire
service at his station down in the city, working twelve
hours shifts, and Hannie spent full days at her desk, catching
up on the all the work she'd put on hold while her life
twisted and turned in ways she couldn't have imagined just a
few weeks before.

The weather was mild, with days in the mid-twenties and
nights cool enough to pull on an extra blanket, but everyone
in Reynolds Ridge and surrounding towns knew the reprieve
wouldn't last. The Bureau of Meteorology had forecast that
the heat and northerly winds would return, sweeping across
from the north of Western Australia and the Northern
Territory in a giant arc, so she took the opportunity to get
some things done. People living in bushfire areas checked the
weather more often they checked their Facebook news feeds,
to judge if today was the day they had to take extra precautions to protect their property, to make sure their petrol
tanks were full, to ensure their animals could be evacuated if
they needed to get out in a hurry and if they themselves

should get in their cars, pack up their valuables and leave.

Hannie took the opportunity to take Ted to his vet's appointment in the nearby town of Uraidla, and Hannie was relieved when the vet told her with a warm smile that Ted's knee was now looking good and that he could be let off the leash to wander so he could get some exercise and restore muscle tone in his leg. It hard been hard, although necessary, to follow doctor's orders when it came to restricting Ted's movements, but it had clearly worked. As soon as they'd got home from the appointment at the clinic, she'd helped him down from the back seat of her four-wheel drive and Ted had trotted off immediately, sniffing every plant and shrub and tree around her cottage, his tail wagging as if he was smelling everything for the very first time. She loved seeing him so free after weeks of such restriction. He was relishing his freedom and Ted wasn't the only one who was pleased that his medical treatment was over.

Hannie had called the hospital and tried to speak to her Aunt Mandy, but she'd been out of her room having some more tests at the time, so Hannie had left another message. When Mandy didn't call back, Hannie wondered if she was getting the messages at all. So Hannie sent flowers and a card, wishing her aunt well and sending hugs and kisses from Zelda and the girls. Every day, when Hannie fed the animals, she checked over at her aunt's house and wondered if Mandy would ever return to the place she loved so much. Alice had remained silent and uncommunicative, so Hannie figured

Alice was still furious with her. She'd done a lot of thinking about the situation, and figured her best move was to wait to hear from Mandy. The balls were in her court on this one. It was her health and her life and her property.

To distract herself from thinking about Dylan and the sex she was missing out on, Hannie got busy at her desk. She put the finishing touches to the piece she'd designed for Beck, and worked on six other commissions she had waiting. She restored and polished a pair of diamond earrings. She'd created a bracelet from a vintage necklace, and crafted a ring with a row of diamonds from a few separate, much-loved but well-worn pieces. She made appointments with her clients to drop off the pieces and check fittings. She browsed the catalogues from a couple of gem dealers she knew and let her imagination run ahead of her. Thinking time was precious in a creative industry like hers, and she tried as hard as she could to clear her mind of everything else to let the ideas flow.

When she needed a break, she slipped on a pair of jeans and her steel-capped boots and hauled an extension ladder out from Mandy's shed to clean the gutters on her cottage and on Mandy's house. The high winds of the previous week had filled them with crisply dry, long and thin gum leaves, which had flown through the air and clogged downpipes. It would quickly become a hazard if there was a fire nearby, as the high winds could pick up burning embers that would flicker and fly through the air like glowing fireflies, and set the leaves alight. A fire in a gutter would in a matter of minutes spread and engulf a house. It was monotonous, albeit important work, and as she moved the ladder from place to place, climbed it, and flicked out the leaves with a heavy glove, her mind was full of Dylan.

She wondered if he was at the fire station and what he was doing. Was he involved in some training or educating some new recruits? Was he out in the truck at the scene of a car accident, reaching people from the wreckage or cleaning up fuel or chemical spills? Was he at the scene of a house fire, caused by a faulty air-conditioner? Or was he back at base, waiting, on edge, for the next call.

And was he thinking about her as much as she was thinking about him?

That first night they'd spent together, she hadn't stayed, even though she'd wanted to. Ted was waiting for her and she'd had to go home and let him out for a pitstop, so it had been just past midnight, after Dylan made her the best toasted ham and cheese sandwich on the planet that they had sauntered out to her car.

He'd held her hand. It seemed so old-fashioned but it had felt so right. She hadn't wanted to let go of him, and clearly he'd felt the same. When she'd been ravenously wolfing down the sandwich he'd made for her – sex always made her hungry – he'd pulled her into his lap and held her while she ate. As they'd been standing by her car, her about to leave, he'd slipped his arms around her and kissed her again, with a hunger she hadn't ever felt in a man.

"You really have to go, huh?"

It had been almost pitch-black out there in Dylan's yard, with only the light from the kitchen windows and the back door spilling out over the veranda. Above, there a canopy of stars which looked as if someone had strung fairy lights from tree to tree. "It's Ted. I left him inside."

"Damn that hound," Dylan said, smiling down at her.

"Hey. Don't talk about my dog that way, Knight. He's my most loyal companion."

Dylan had chuckled. "Well, he better get used to the fact that he's gonna have some competition there."

She thought back to that moment, to the long, hot kiss that followed, and smiled.

She flicked a clump of dead gum leaves on to the ground and they fluttered and scattered on to the grass and gravel below. Dylan Knight. How was it possible that she was already crazy about him? She climbed down the ladder and picked up a rake, gathering all the leaves into a pile for depositing in the green bins. Just before she'd got in her car, Dylan had promised he'd see her on the last night of his four-shift stint.

That was tomorrow night.

And she couldn't wait.

ON THE EVENING of the third day of his four-shift stretch,

Dylan caught up with his twin brother Caleb. They worked in different fire stations in the city and were on different shifts, so seeing each other was usually a quick beer or a morning coffee in between night shift or long day shifts. But tonight, they'd actually managed to wrangle time enough for a meal at an old pub in Maylands, tucked away in the Adelaide suburbs between the city and the hills. It was an historic place, built of local bluestone, and had a great front bar, with walls covered with framed sporting memorabilia of local football and cricket legends.

Caleb came back to their table with a couple of beers and a bag of chips. "Here, open those."

Dylan split the pack and they tucked in. "Salt and vinegar?" Dylan asked as he crunched a chip. "You know I hate salt and vinegar."

"That's why I got 'em. Caleb looked happy and relaxed, and as fit as a professional athlete. His hair was cut in almost the same style, short all over, but his was brown and Dylan's was blond. They weren't identical, but there was no mistaking them as brothers. Both broad shouldered, strong, six foot three.

"So how's tricks, little bro?" Dylan had always liked to rub it in that he was the older of the two and, while it was only by twelve minutes, he liked to think it gave him some moral authority over his slightly younger brother.

"Good," Caleb said.

"Been out on your new bike yet?"

Caleb sipped his beer. "I love it. It runs like a dream. I did Mt. Lofty this morning, twice, and it didn't skip a beat." Mt Lofty was the highest peak in the Adelaide Hills and dedicated cyclists did the run a few times a week. "You should come with me next time. It'd do you good to get some fresh air."

"What are you talking about? I live in the fresh air."

"Cycling's great. You should come try it."

Dylan laughed. The hills had been full of cyclists a few weeks ago during the Tour Down Under, the international road race which brought world class cyclists to Adelaide. Each January, the city went mad for lycra. Dylan would never be one of them. Cycling just wasn't his thing.

"You know what's so good about being nonidentical twins, Caleb? It means we don't have to like the same shit. Give me a run in the great outdoors any day. Or why don't you come up to my place and help me clear some dead trees around the property? Lugging those around and chopping them up for firewood will give you a work-out."

"I keep meaning to come up and have a look. How are things up there at Reynolds Ridge? What's it like being back?" Caleb sipped his beer, and then leaned his elbows on the table.

"It's almost stopped feeling like Mum and Dad's house." Dylan smiled. "It's such a great part of the world. I can't believe I stayed away so long." From the corner of his eye, Dylan saw a message pop up on his phone. Was it Hannie?

"You expecting a message?" Caleb craned his neck and tried to look.

"Nope." He shrugged. "Maybe."

"Okay, spill, bro." He put down his beer. "Who is she?"

Dylan pushed the phone to the side. It wasn't her. It was one of his buddies from the station looking to swap a shift in the next month. He'd get back to him later, try to help out of he could.

"What?"

Caleb peered across the table at his brother. "You're mighty distracted, mate. I was asking you, who the woman is."

Dylan felt the smile coming on before he could contain it. It was never a good idea to show too much enthusiasm for anything in front of Caleb, who had a way of ribbing him about any damn thing. He still brought up the time he beat Dylan in their year six one hundred metre race at their primary school's sports carnival. But... fuck it. Dylan wanted to talk about Hannie and how he felt about her. How it had been so crazy so quick. How, when he was with her, he didn't want to let go of her. And how it had been three days since he'd seen her, kissed, held her, and that he was about to go nuts from missing her.

"You remember Hannie Reynolds, from Reynolds Ridge? From school?"

Caleb thought on the question. "The one with the purple hair? The one who lived at the back of our place? The one you kissed at that party?"

Dylan smiled at the memory. "Yeah, that's her. Her hair's dark now, you know, normal. And kind of long, which she pulls up into this bun at the top of her head. And she's a jeweller."

Caleb looked around in amazement. "What the fuck? You've gone and got yourself a woman – and it's Hannie Reynolds – and this is the first time I hear about it? You're putting the bro code in serious doubt here. I want details. What's been going on? How many times and where? Is it good?"

Caleb was going to get far fewer details than he expected. This thing with Hannie was too important to be talking about while shooting the shit at the pub. "It's only been …" How long had it been? A couple of weeks? "Not that long."

"I know you. You're looking all sooky la-la. This isn't just some hookup, is it?"

"Nope. This could be something good, Caleb. Hannie's pretty amazing. She lives on that old cottage at her aunt Mandy's place; you know, the one we used to think was haunted when we were kids. It's been done up and she's running her own business from there, in between looking after her Aunt Mandy's place and all her animals while she's in hospital."

Caleb held up a hand. "Whoa. You talking about Mandy, Alice's mother?"

"Yeah."

"What happened to her? Why's she in hospital?"

Dylan wouldn't normally have told anyone such personal information but since their mother had already called him to ask about it, it was clear the news was already out "She's got Parkinson's."

"Oh, shit. That sucks."

"She's been pretty good for a while but she's had a couple of falls and they're running all kinds of tests on her in hospital. Alice wants her to sell up and move into some kind of care, which means Hannie will be kicked out of her house."

Caleb sat back. "How do you know all this stuff?"

"It's her life, Caleb. I care about her and what happens to her."

"Obviously."

Dylan glanced at his phone again.

Caleb rolled his eyes. "Why don't you just call her, you dipshit."

"Don't call me a dipshit, dipshit."

"Go on. Clearly you've got a thing for this woman. Remember what that incorrigible cousin of ours said at our grandfather's funeral?" Caleb lifted his beer and announced grandiosely. "'To getting laid and fighting fires'."

Dylan didn't clink his brother's glass. "Fuck you. I'm not toasting to that."

"So this Hannie. Is this really something serious? Already?"

"Yeah, it is," Dylan said.

Caleb smiled.

"Wait a minute. You getting any that I don't know about?"

It wasn't lost on Dylan that his little brother completely ignored his question.

"Here's cheers, big bro."

AFTER DINNER WAS over, Dylan drove up into the hills and home towards Reynolds Ridge. It was twilight, the sun setting in the west cast a warm glow through the trees and the valleys, and it was quiet. As he approached Mandy's place, situated close to the road and on the high side, he saw something unfamiliar out the front.

A *For Sale* sign. He checked in his rearview mirror that the road was clear behind him before slamming on his brakes and taking the driveway down to Hannie's cottage. She was outside on the lawn, throwing a tennis ball a few feet for Ted to fetch. He pulled up, jumped out of the car, and strode over to her.

She looked up. Her eyes were red and her face tear streaked.

"What the fuck?" he called out. "I just saw the sign."

Ted dropped the ball at Hannie's feet. She bent down to pick it up and rolled it across the lawn. "It went up today. She's selling."

"She can't do that. She can't order her own mother around like a child. Mandy has to fight this."

Hannie looked up at him with the saddest eyes he'd ever seen. He fought the urge to take her into his arms and whisper words of comfort to her, to reassure her that everything was going to be all right.

"It's Mandy's decision."

"I don't believe it," Dylan scoffed.

"It's true," Hannie replied, wiping her eyes. "She told me herself, Dylan. I got a call this morning. She thanked me for the flowers I'd sent and apologised for not calling me. She'd been a bit too upset about everything to speak to anyone. You see"—Hannie paused, as if she was trying to take in the news as well—"the results from her tests aren't good. Mandy has agreed with Alice that she needs to move into a place where she can get the best care. This place is available to the highest bidder."

Dylan's mind was spinning. He was used to taking control, to running teams, to thinking of every possibility. He had to come up with something. For Hannie's sake.

"Can you buy this place?"

Hannie shook her head. "I don't have that kind of money. And anyway, it's not what I want for my future."

"Maybe the new owners will let you stay on as a tenant?"

"I got the place in return for looking after Mandy and her animals. The new owners will want full market rent and might even turn the cottage into a bed and breakfast. They'll want me out. I'll find somewhere else."

Dylan couldn't hold back now. He went to Hannie, pulled her in close, tried to ignore Ted slobbering on his shoe, and held her. He kissed the top of her head.

"I don't know what I'm going to do about Zelda and the girls. Do you want some chickens and a goat?" she asked.

"Let me think. No."

"I'll talk to Ted's vet. She's in the next town. She might know someone who'll take them."

Hannie was going to be evicted from her home and she was thinking about a stinky, head-butting goat and the chooks?

"Let's go inside, Hannie."

WHEN THE MOON was full in the sky, Dylan and Hannie made love. They barely moved from the bed that night and except for Dylan's early morning trip to pick up Ted from Hannie's place, they stayed between the sheets for the whole of the next day and night. Thirty-six whole hours of love-making, laughing, sleeping, watching movies, drinking wine, and eating. It was like the best holiday Hannie had ever had.

It was definitely the best sex she'd ever had.

He was a keeper. She just had to figure out how to tell him.

Chapter Fifteen

DYLAN WOKE WHEN his pager went off.

It buzzed on the bedside table by the left hand side of his bed and he blinked his eyes open at the sound of it. Even though the buzzing was quiet, he swore he would hear it in the middle of the deepest sleep when he was on standby during an Australian summer. Hannie was still tucked into him, her head on his shoulder and an arm across his chest, sound asleep. For half a second, only half, he wished he could ignore it and stay in bed with her all day like this, naked, sated, every inch of him still alive at her touch.

He wanted to watch her while she slept, for just a moment longer. Her face was serene, which was a marked difference from what he'd seen in her a couple of days ago. Her pale skin, a smattering of faint freckles on her pert nose, her full lips parted slightly as she breathed. He almost couldn't bear to look away.

Two nights with her and he was gone. He wanted so much more of this he could barely find the words, and he would, soon enough, but now he had to answer this page.

He slipped out of bed, slowly, and tried to noiselessly walk into the kitchen to call the Country Fire Service station.

"It's Knight. What's going on?"

"Mate." It was Tim, the head of the incident management team at Dylan's volunteer station. A local organic orchardist, a burly bloke with a long beard, he was exactly the kind of no-bullshit person someone wanted in charge when the shit was hitting the fan. "Arsonists. Bloody bastards. Someone's lit ten fires near Uraidla on Range Road. The winds aren't looking good and four of them are threatening to run out of control."

"I'm on my way."

Dylan ended the call. He only had a minute to grab his fire gear, get into it, and get to the station.

"What's going on?"

He spun around. Hannie was standing in the doorway to the kitchen, half asleep and totally naked, rubbing her eyes, yawning.

He lost his breath.

"Dylan?"

"I've got to go, Hannie. Ten fires at Uraidla. An arsonist, they reckon." He crossed the room, swept her up into his arms, and kissed her senseless.

Her arms around him were like a vice. "Stay safe, Dylan," she said. Her morning voice was still croaky but her eyes were wide and alert.

"You'll be okay?"

"Of course. My car's here. I'll get dressed and head back now."

"I'll call when I can." He reluctantly let her go.

She grabbed his hand as he walked away and kissed the top of it.

"Hannie …" He started but couldn't finish.

"Go," she said. And he was out the door.

ONCE SHE'D GOT Ted home, she sat in her kitchen, was glued to the radio. She'd lived through fires before, so many she'd lost count, but there was something about this one that seemed real bad, real quick. As the morning wore on, reports were getting worse.

The fire front was getting bigger.

It was burning out of control on all fronts, with a perimeter of more than forty kilometres and the fierce northerlies of up to ninety kilometres an hour were fanning the ferocious blaze south easterly – right towards Reynolds Ridge.

Hannie had already changed out of her T-shirt and shorts and was wearing jeans and steel-capped boots. She had a protective fire coat on the stool at the end of the bench, and her most precious things – photos, passports and other official documents, her laptop, and the pieces she'd been working on for her clients – were already in the back of her four-wheel drive, collected in a plastic tub. Ted was inside with her, unsettled and anxious, pacing the kitchen, as he always did on severe weather days. She'd walked up to Mandy's place and shooed the chooks into the henhouse and tied Zelda up closer to the house. Her mobile was fully charged and tucked in the front pocket of her jeans and she had plenty of water in the car. She'd checked the generator too, and the pumps to the water tanks.

All she could do now was wait for the call to evacuate.

She drank some water and had a turkey sandwich and some fruit for lunch. While she didn't feel hungry in the slightest, if things got hairy it might be a while before she would eat, and she might need every scrap of energy she could muster to get out of there safely and head to refuge. She turned up her radio, tuned in to the national broadcaster, the ABC.

There was an alarm sound which brought her to attention and then the grave newsreaders voice began.

"This warning has been issued in relation to the current fire event southeast of Uraidla in the Adelaide Hills. There is a heightened level of threat in the townships of Uraidla, Woods Peak and Reynolds Ridge. Conditions are changing and you need to start taking action now to protect you and your family. If you live in the area but are away from home, it may not be safe to return to your property."

Hannie went outside and looked up into the sky. It was clear around her and all the way up to the top of Reynolds Ridge, but when she looked to the northeast, she gasped. Gigantic plumes of white smoke were looming in the sky, so white they might look like a billowing cloud to someone who wasn't familiar with fires. They almost looked like a volcanic eruption. Closer to the ground, the clouds of smoke were grey and heavy, and Hannie knew what it was. The fire was fierce and huge and only getting bigger. The smoke must have been as high as a kilometre in the sky.

She wasn't going to take risks. This was the time to leave. Fires could get out of control in what seemed like minutes and, if that was the case, she had not time to spare. She ran to her shed and switched on the pump. Moments later, her sprinklers were on, and would soak everything around her cottage in the hope that it wouldn't burn. She ran up the driveway to do the same to Mandy's house. She'd prepared the property as much as she could and now hoped this emergency measure would do the trick. She stopped and patted Zelda, who was bleating in distress.

"Don't worry you old goat. I'll be back for you. Give me a minute to get Ted. I'm afraid the girls are going to have to stay."

Hannie ran through the water exploding into the air like a fountain in front of Mandy's place and made it back to hers, panting with the adrenaline rush of fear coursing through her veins. She grabbed her handbag and her car keys from the kitchen table and looked around.

"Ted?"

He wasn't in his bed in the corner of the room. She ran down the hallway, calling his name, but he didn't come. She pushed open the back door and looked across the yard. She whistled, called his name again, but he was nowhere to be seen.

"Ted!" She shouted this time, scared out of her wits, scanning all around her, and when she looked to the west, her heart almost stopped. There were flames in the distance, maybe one kilometre away, bright orange fingers of destruction on the top of the hill, licking skywards. Hannie smelt the smoke.

She tried to breathe. She was ready. She had everything in motion. She knew how to get out of Reynolds Ridge. All she had to do now was find Ted and get out of there.

AT INCIDENT COMMAND, Dylan was pacing back and forth. The room, set up in an old stone building on the side of a road outside Uraidla, had a large shed to the side which housed the fire trucks when they weren't out on the road, and a communications room where the fire response was coordinated. Next door, the volunteers of the local Country Women's Association had already set up a food station, and were cutting sandwiches by the dozen, preparing to feed the hungry volunteers who would return to the station during the day for a break, for water, to prepare themselves to go back out there and fight the fire. Inside the station, there were people busily doing the jobs they'd been assigned to help protect the communities they lived in and loved, and the people who lived in it. With so many volunteers and trucks out fighting the blaze from their station and others all over the hills, plus coordinating with the police chopper overhead and the water bombers if they were needed, this was the centre of the response.

Dylan had just arrived, five minutes after held got the message on his pager. "I swear, Tim, if you don't let me out on a truck, I'll—"

Tim held up a hand. "Mate. My regular second in command got trapped at his place by a fallen tree and now he's fighting to save his own property and his neighbours' from going up. I need someone here I can trust and you're it."

Dylan gritted his teeth. "Fuck. Not Max and Shirley Norris."

Tim nodded. "Yep. Last thing I heard, they've lost everything. Home. Sheds. Even their bloody tractor."

Dylan's resolve strengthened. "Okay. Let me know what you need."

Tim handed him a mobile phone. "Tell the bigwigs in the Emergency Management Council meeting down in Adelaide that we need the water bomber. Right now. The front has extended to fifty kilometres and we've got a whole lot of small towns in the path of it."

"Which towns?" Dylan followed Tim to the map of the local area pinned to the wall.

"Uraidla. Woods Peak. Reynolds Ridge. Maysville."

It might have been forty two degrees Celsius outside in

the blazing north wind, but Dylan felt ice cold.

He looked up to the white board next to the map, scanned it for the number he needed and dialled.

FIVE MINUTES LATER, Hannie was frantic. She scoured almost every inch of the property, from the road which almost met Mandy's front door, to inside the sheds where she'd turned on the generators. Ted loved to rummage around in there hunting the scent of feral cats.

The only place she hadn't looked was the creek bed at the bottom of the valley, where Reynolds Ridge rose up, with Dylan's place at the top of it. Damn it. Ted had been kept away from his beloved creek for a month while he'd been recovering and she could bet that was where he was.

The smell of the fire burning was stronger now. It must be getting closer. Clouds of smoke wafted over here and brought with it a light ash, like snow. She had to move fast. She jogged down the incline towards the creek bed, which she guessed would be dry as there hadn't been a decent rain in months, took care to navigate the shrubs and stones in the ground which could easily trip her. The last thing she needed was a sprained ankle when she was getting ready to get the hell out of there.

Then she heard him.

"Ted!" she shouted and waited.

The wind had picked up and it was fierce now, frying

everything it touched, tearing leaves from trees and flicking them across the gully into her face, stinging her skin. The noise was so loud she couldn't be sure where his bark was coming from. She called again and he answered and she followed the plaintive sound until she finally reached the bottom of the creek bed.

"Ted…" He was covered in dust and sticks and stones and when he saw her, he didn't leap up and run to her, but he sat on his butt, his eyes lowered, his ears drooping. Hannie's heart sank. What was wrong with him? When she reached him, she threw her arms around him and sobbed. Her Ted. Her poor, slobbery Ted. He licked her face and burrowed into the crook of her neck, whimpering.

"You big duffer," she cried out. "What have you done?" She slipped a finger under his collar and tried to get him to stand, but he flopped back down on to his butt. She tried again but he seemed to have lost feeling in his hind legs. She looked up to the sky. It was a swirling cloud. There was only one thing to do.

She was going to have to carry Ted back up the steep incline to her car. At a weight of forty kilograms, it was going to test her, but she had no other choice. She wasn't living without Ted.

"Come on," she said, taking a deep breath. The smoke in the air almost choked her. "We're going to get out of here." She slipped one arm under his belly and the other around his back and lifted him, using her knee to get him higher so she had more control. She made it ten feet before stopping. She looked up. There was at least a hundred feet to go. She tried again, got a little further. And then lifted him again and again.

When Hannie was halfway up, she heard someone calling. She looked up, tried to flick away the sweat that had drizzled into her eyes, tried to hear above the roar of the wind.

"Hannie!"

Chapter Sixteen

"HANNIE? WHAT ARE you doing down there?"

Hannie looked up, squinted, tried to make out who it was. "Mel?"

"Yeah, it's me. We've closed up the café and we're checking on everyone on our way out. What's going on?"

Hannie lifted Ted again and then froze. A pain stabbed across her whole lower back, as if she'd stuck her fingers into an electric socket. It contorted every muscle in her abdomen and she gasped.

"Oh… fuck." Her breath escaped her and she couldn't seem to draw any back into her lungs.

"Kaz, come quick," Mel yelled over her shoulder. Mel and Kaz, who owned the famous Organic Café on the main road running through Reynolds Ridge – the only cafe in Reynolds Ridge – were also her neighbours from a few clicks down the road.

"Something's wrong with Ted," Hannie called out as Mel scampered down to her. Kaz was only a moment behind. "He can't seem to move. He had surgery on one knee a few weeks ago." Hannie stopped, gasping for breath and flinching at the agonising pain. She tried to straighten her back but couldn't. She suddenly felt hot and cold all at once and fought the strong urge to vomit.

Mel looked her up and down with concern. "You're white as a sheet, Hannie. It looks like you can't walk either. Don't lift him again. We'll take him. You wait here. We'll come back for you." Mel and Kaz stood on each side of Ted and lifted him up. They bent at the knees like people who knew how to protect themselves from a lifting injury, something Hannie realised she hadn't done, and she watched them move up the hill as they moved out of sight over the top of the incline. A few moments later, Mel and Kaz had scrambled down back to her.

"I'm all packed and ready to go but I couldn't leave him. I couldn't." Tears welled in Hannie's eyes, from fear or pain, or both. "Thank you."

"It's nothing." Mel and Kaz exchanged a serious look. "Can you move at all?"

"I'll try." Hannie took a step. Another stab of pain. She gasped and reached out for support from her friends' shoulders. "It hurts like fuck, excuse the French. But we have to get out of here. The fire's close. I saw the flames over the ridge."

Kaz nodded. "That's why we're getting out. It's headed right for us, Hannie."

Hannie summoned every bit of strength she had and

clenched her jaw so tight it ached. She took another step, half carried up the hill by her friends. Each footfall was like a knife across her back. It took a five full minutes, but they finally made it. When Hannie saw Ted in Mel and Kaz's four-wheel drive, leaning out the window barking like a maniac at the sight of her, fresh tears welled in her eyes.

"You're coming with us," Kaz said. "There's no way you can drive. We've got room."

They led Hannie to their vehicle and opened one of the rear passenger doors, slowly urging her inside. She half expected Ted to leap all over her but he was secured with his leash to the headrest so he wouldn't go bouncing around the car as they fled.

"All my stuff is in my car," Hannie said urgently.

"I've got it." Mel raced over and grabbed the two tubs of possessions Hannie had loaded earlier that day and stowed them in the back of her own.

Hannie felt dizzy but was scared to close her eyes. She stared out the car window at her cottage. Would it still be standing when the fire was finally out? She couldn't know. She couldn't think about it now.

They had to get out.

"Okay. Let's go." Kaz started the vehicle and it made a throaty rumble as she circled and headed back up the gravel driveway to the main road. The sprinklers were still going around Mandy's house and Hannie choked up at the thought of Mandy losing her beloved place twice.

"Wait!" she called sharply. "We've got to get Zelda."

"Zelda?" Mel asked over the back seat.

"Mandy's goat. I don't think we can save all the chooks – there's too many of them – but we have to get Mandy's goat."

TWENTY MINUTES LATER, Hannie, Mel, Kaz, Ted, and Zelda arrived at the evacuation centre at a community oval in the nearby town of Waters Gully. It was a football club in the winter, but in summer it became a makeshift evacuation point where people from surrounding townships could gather safely out of harm's way. Sometimes roads were blocked by fallen trees, which made getting out of the hills impossible. Other times, like today, the smoke haze was so thick that they couldn't see ten feet in front of them. The large oval, with its well-watered grass, was a safe haven and the local emergency services had set up there to care for people.

Zelda and Ted were tethered to Mel and Kaz's four-wheel drive, eyeing each other suspiciously. Ted sat quietly, his back legs still giving him some pain. Mel had walked over to the first aid station to see if anyone had anything for Hannie to take to settle her back. She should probably be in hospital with a knock-her-out pain-killing injection, but she was hardly a priority at the moment when there the possibility of burns injuries – or worse.

"Here." Mel had returned with a portion of a blister pack in her hand.

"What's that?" Kaz asked, staring at it like it was a dead spider.

"It's paracetamol."

"You're kidding," Mel replied with a furious tone. "That won't even touch the sides. Hannie could have a slipped disc, for god's sake."

Hannie was listening from the back seat. They'd managed to lower her so she was lying down, her steel-capped booted feet dangling outside. If she didn't breathe much and stayed completely still, it didn't hurt quite so much. She was working hard to keep her breathing constant so the panic didn't set in. A slipped disc? She didn't even know what that meant but the pain was telling her it was something serious. If Mel and Kaz hadn't come along when they had, if they hadn't bothered to check where she was … Hannie couldn't think. Mandy was safe in the city and now she and Ted were safe. Her angels – Mel and Kaz – were fussing over Ted and Zelda, making sure they had a bucket of water to share in the heat.

"You right there, Hannie?" Mel was by her feet looking into the car.

"I'm good. Well, I'll be fine."

"Let me get something to put under your head. It'll make you more comfortable."

"And roll up that blanket there and tuck it under her

knees," Kaz added.

Hannie swallowed the tablets they had given her with some lukewarm bottled water and thought about Dylan. She'd stared at her phone for a full five minutes waiting for a signal to magically appear but there was nothing.

Where was he?

IN THE FIRE station command centre at Uraidla, Dylan was standing with Tim listening to reports coming in from the crews out fighting the fires.

Tim looked grave. "When did the Emergency Management Centre say the water bomber would arrive?"

Dylan checked the time. "About now. I tried to kick some arse, but we're not the only front. There are fires in the plains north of Adelaide. A fire truck's been lost on the Yorke Peninsula with ten crew injured. And six civilians are missing, mate." Just relaying the information to Tim had Dylan's stomach dropping into his boots.

He'd been hearing all the field reports for an hour now. It was a shit storm out there in every direction. The fire in the hills was uncontrollable and raging, gobbling up homes and businesses in its path like a voracious beast whose hunger couldn't be assuaged. The flames had jumped back-burned fire breaks in ten locations and were now spreading into the national park which ran alongside his property and Mandy's. Dylan felt useless. He fished his phone out of his pocket.

Still no signal.

Hannie would have left by now. She'd grown up with the threat of fires. She'd said herself how prepared she was and he'd seen it around the property. It had been a matter of pride, in fact, that she was capable of looking after herself and Mandy and Mandy's property. She would have got out. He was sure of it.

But until he saw her with his own eyes, held her, kissed, told her he loved her, he couldn't rest.

"Hey, Knight."

Dylan looked up. Tim was holding a phone to his ear. His expression was grave. "One of my crew's reporting that a house has been lost on the south end of Reynolds Ridge. That's where you are, right?"

"I'm up on the north side, on top of the ridge." Pain contorted his jaw as he clenched it closed. "There's a property on the other side of the gully, a big stone house and a cottage." He drew in a deep breath. "Which one is it?"

Tim relayed the question to his caller. He listened, waited.

It felt to Dylan like it was ten years before Tim answered.

"It's the big stone house and the cottage. Mandy Reynolds' place. Looks like it's all gone. The fire moved across from the national park too quick. There was nothing they could do."

Dylan's hands became fists. A headache throbbed behind his eyes that almost blinded him. He had a duty to Tim, their colleagues on the trucks and every volunteer out there fighting the fire. But he needed to know.

"Tim. Let me go. I need to make sure Hannie got out."

"Nope," Tim said sternly. "I'm sorry, mate, but I can't let you go. Hannie's smart. I've known her since high school, too. She will have got out hours ago. We've already got people injured and others are missing. It won't be on my conscience to lose you too, you mad bastard." Tim walked to Dylan, put a firm hand on his shoulder and squeezed. "Keep listening to the reports from the crews out at the fire front. When it's safe to go, you can go. But in the meantime, find out where the fuck the water bomber is, will you?"

DYLAN WAS OUT of his mind, but he couldn't show it to anyone at incident command. Every single person there feared for someone, for their own homes, for local businesses, for people they knew and loved in their communities. What made his terror worse than theirs? He had to pull himself up. He needed to do his job, to back up Tim, to pull crews out of places that were too dangerous and send them to other locations where they could do some good. The burden of sending men and women into a fire was one he'd never felt before, and the responsibility felt like a lead weight in the pit of his stomach. Everyone single person on the fire trucks had been well-trained, but fires had no logic or reason; they could jump from house to house to house along a road, incinerating every property but one. They could leave one animal untouched in a paddock when every other one around it was lost.

Fires were cruel, unrelenting, unpredictable and hungry.

He tried not to think about Hannie. And Ted. And that stupid, head-butting goat.

Her cottage was gone. Mandy's house was gone. She'd lost everything.

Another pointless look at this phone. Still no reception.

Where was she?

Chapter Seventeen

T HE FIRE RAGED for the next twenty-four hours, through the night and into the next day, running up gullies and along hilltop ridges, scorching tracts of grassed farm land, cherry and apple orchards, and a great swath of the national park in Reynolds Ridge.

At the evacuation point, more help had arrived and tents had been erected, with mattresses and blankets inside, so all the families could have some privacy and get some sleep. The volunteer ambulance officers had wangled Hannie a tent so she could lie down and Mel and Kaz and Ted had moved in, too. Zelda was quite enjoying the grass of the oval and some of the local children, who'd been evacuated from their homes, had adopted her. The old goat was in heaven.

It was a surreal place to be, as if they were in the eye of a storm. Silver-haired men behind a row of barbecues had been working day and night, cooking sausages and eggs and bacon for all those who were at the evacuation centre. The smell of it wafted through the entire makeshift campground, battling with the smell of the fire and burning gums.

Hannie hadn't left her tent, except to go to the bathroom in the football club's change rooms on the edge of the oval and Ted was at her side. Her back was still agony, although some stronger painkillers from the ambulance crew had helped. There had been some pressure for her to be taken to hospital, but she'd refused, pretended the pain wasn't as bad as it was. She couldn't leave until she knew what had happened to her house and until she knew that Dylan was safe.

"Hannie?" Kaz pushed aside one of the front flaps on the tent and peered inside.

"Yeah?"

"You're awake." Kaz and Mel came inside and sat down beside Hannie.

She lifted her head to look at them but could only last a second or too. "You saying I was asleep?"

"You've slept a bit. It must be the drugs for your back," Mel said quietly. "Which is probably a good thing."

"There's something I need to tell you," Kaz said, and when she reached for Hannie's hand, Hannie knew.

"Oh no."

Mel and Kaz looked at each other, both crying. "Your place and Mandy's. They're gone."

Hannie reached her other hand out for Ted and urged him close. She'd faced this so many times before in her life but it was real now. Her home. All her possessions, except what crammed into the two plastic tubs in the back of Mel and Kaz's car. Her jewellery tools and her bits and pieces of gems and metals and beads. Her drawings and sketches. Her clothes, her books, her CDs, her saucepans. She didn't even have a knife and fork left to her name. Her bed, where she and Dylan had made love just a week ago.

It was all ashes.

How had her whole world collapsed in on her so quickly? And Mandy. Oh, god. She would be heartbroken.

"Hannie, do you understand what I just said?" Kaz asked.

Hannie nodded. She felt the warm sting of tears running down her face and into her ears. This was all too much. She closed her eyes and sobbed.

AT THE FIRE station command, Dylan had just got word that the Reynolds Ridge fire had burnt pretty much everything in its path heading south and had already moved ten kilometres towards Maysville.

"Am I good to go?" he asked Tim.

"Go. Take the Kings track to the north of your place and you should be right. But don't be long. I've still got crews everywhere."

Dylan bolted to his car and, as per Tim's advice, took the rutted Kings track around the back of his place to the top of Reynolds Ridge. It wasn't used by regular road users any more but was regularly graded and cleared in case it was needed for emergency access. The hills were full of winding roads that were often the only way in and out of a place. So the back tracks were needed if trees had blocked roads or fallen power lines had made them life-threatening.

Dylan noticed the singed trees on either side of the track. When he turned a corner, he looked up ahead and saw his place. His heart thudded in his chest. It was still there. The flood of relief was indescribable. He pulled into his driveway and leapt out of his car. He jogged around to the front of the house and looked across the valley.

There was smoke rising from two stone buildings.

He took off down into the gully, slowly jogging, checking where his feet fell for hazards which could bring him down. This was the quickest way across to Mandy's property. At the bottom of the gully, the empty creek bed was dry as a bone. He crossed it, and began climbing up the other side, using his hands to crawl up. He was almost there when he could smell burning fuel and melted plastic.

When he made it to the top, he propped his hands on his hips to get his breath. When he lifted his eyes, there was devastation. Hannie's beautifully restored cottage was now nothing but a tall brick chimney, miraculously still standing, and half destroyed stone walls. They looked like ancient Roman ruins in the smouldering earth. Sheets of twisted galvanised iron lay on the ground inside the half-destroyed stone walls, as if they had toppled from a pile, and wisps of white smoke were swirling into the air from whatever was still smouldering underneath.

He walked over to the ruin and that was when he saw Hannie's four-wheel drive. The tyres had melted into black pools on the dirt; the rims were scorched and sitting flat on the ground. The smell of the burnt plastic interior burning was chemical and choking and overwhelming. Dylan pulled a kerchief from around his neck up over his mouth.

Why the fuck was her car still here?

"Hannie?" he called out, walking faster now, looking inside the windows of the car for a sign, please god, that she hadn't been in there.

"Hannie?" he called again, louder this time, more frantic, his heartbeat thudding in his ears and his legs like jelly. He forced them to take him over to the house where he stumbled through the empty space where the wooden front door had been. A half-melted saucepan sat on top of what might have been her kitchen sink. Glass jars had exploded and there were shards everywhere. He couldn't see that anything was left of her wooden kitchen table or chairs. He walked through to where her workshop had been and it was a broken, shattered mess. Her desk was gone but when he looked down into the grey and white ashes, he half-recognised something. He nudged them with his boot. Her weird jeweller's glasses. Dylan bent to pick them up. Melted almost beyond recognition, he kept them in his hand.

Why was her car still in the driveway?

Had she run somewhere to try to escape? Dylan looked around the property, from the creek bed to Mandy's house.

He jogged across to the ruin and searched, in case she'd taken refuge there. Did Mandy have a cellar? Had Hannie hidden down there? No, Hannie would know that people suffocated in cellars from the lack of oxygen. He stumbled back out in to Mandy's yard.

This time he yelled at the top of his lungs, screeching so hard it hurt his throat. "Hannie!"

There was nothing. There was no birdsong.

There was no bark from Ted.

There was no response from Hannie.

BACK AT THE station, Dylan reported in to Tim. "Two homes destroyed. Mandy's place and Hannie's cottage. There's nothing left."

Tim swore. "And no sign of her?"

The weight of what he needed to say was too heavy. All Dylan could do was shake his head instead.

"Did you check if she made it to the evacuation centre down the road? She might be there, right?"

Dylan met Tim's worried eyes. "Her car… her car was in the yard. Burnt out."

Tim's face fell. "Fuck."

"You got a thing with Hannie?"

"Yeah."

"Sorry mate. I really am. But you'd better list her as a missing person."

HANNIE HAD MANAGED to move slowly and painfully across the oval to the line at the barbecue. She was still in a daze, but thought she'd better eat. Some lovely volunteers had moved from tent to tent offering cans of pet foods to families who had brought their much-loved pets with them, so Ted had a full belly and was asleep. He still wouldn't put any weight on his back legs and Hannie figured one of the first things she'd have to do when all this was over was get Ted back to the vet.

She had to pull herself up. When this was all over?

At that moment, Hannie felt as if the nightmare would never be over. She had wanted to set up a studio somewhere new, had been working hard to save so she could make that leap, but now it all seemed lost. How long would it take to start again, to find a new place to live, a new studio, a new desk, new tools?

She didn't even have a change of underwear. That was what a girl needed, right, to start again? A change of underwear and a second pair of shoes. She wiggled her toes inside her steel-capped boots. She was going to get real tired of them real quick.

"Hannie?"

She looked behind her. "Amanda?" Amanda was an old school friend who ran the local supermarket with her husband Peter.

"Oh, Hannie, I'm so sorry. I heard about your place. Mel

and Kaz have been helping me with the catering and they filled me in. It's absolutely devastating."

"Thanks, Amanda." Hannie tried not to flinch in pain at the fierceness of Amanda's embrace. "You and Peter okay?"

"He's out on one of the trucks. It's my job to make sure everyone here is fed and watered."

"That's just as important," Hannie said with a sad smile. "For those of us with nothing left, a humble sausage on a slice of white bread with tomato sauce tastes better than the best Wagyu steak."

Amanda looked around. "Everyone loves a sausage sizzle, that's for sure. Well, hon, if there's anything we can do for you, you just ask, okay?"

"Thanks, Amanda."

Amanda bustled away through the crowd.

Hannie waited patiently in line, glad it wasn't moving too fast for her back's sake, and when she'd snaffled herself a couple of sausages, she headed back over to the tent. Which was when Mel came running towards her, her cheeks flushed, a look of absolute fright in her eyes.

"Hannie." She puffed.

Hannie held out one of her sausages. "I hear you've been working hard in the kitchen. Do you want one of these?"

Mel waved it away. "God, no. I've filled up on bacon and egg sandwiches. And I'm supposed to be a vegetarian. Listen"—she paused, catching her breath—"you need to come with me. I've just found out you've been listed as a missing person."

Hannie froze. "What?"

"Kevin from down the road came by for a coffee and we were chatting and things, going over whose places had been lost and he asked me if I've seen you, and I said, yes, you were sleeping in the tent, and he said that was a relief because you've been listed as missing."

"But I'm right here. How did this happen?"

Mel linked an arm through Hannie's and walked her slowly towards the police car parked on site. "Things have been a little crazy around here, if you haven't noticed. It's what happens when someone can't be contacted."

"But no one's had any mobile reception. I haven't been able to make a call – or get any – in twenty four hours now."

Hannie felt her breathing quicken and become shallower with each breath. Her mother. Oh no. Did her mother think she was dead? And what about Alice and Mandy? Had they been trying to get in touch with her to find out what had happened to the property? And to her?

And Dylan. If he'd been at her place, seen the car she'd had to leave behind, he'd probably be thinking…

"Mel. We've got to tell the police that I'm not missing. That I'm not dead."

Mel let out a half laugh, half sob. "I think that's an excellent idea."

"Dylan," Tim called across the room at the Uraidla fire station command. "Come see this." Tim had just ripped a piece of paper from the printer attached to a laptop on his desk and was waving it around like a flag.

Dylan was searching the map on the wall, studying the red pins that indicted where crews were. He had to bury himself in the work. That was the only way he could not think about Hannie and what might have happened to her. There was a strike crew of five trucks on their way to Maysville and another team heading for Pinky Flat, where an abattoir was under threat of being engulfed. It employed one hundred and twenty local people and the loss of an industry that big in this part of the hills would be devastating. He looked over his shoulder, distracted. "What is it?"

"She's been found."

Dylan froze. "Hannie? She's okay?"

"The cops reckon she's at Waters Gully evacuation centre. She's been hurt, although exactly how is a little unclear from this, but this police report says she's safe."

Dylan stared at Tim. At that moment, words failed him. For a day and a night, he'd hoped for the best but thought the worst. Plenty of people said plenty of prayers in bushfires and it made no difference. They still died and their families still grieved and broken hearts never mended.

But he didn't have a broken heart. He hadn't let himself go there and, now, as it beat like a bass drum in his chest, he had a full heart, full of love for Hannie Reynolds.

"Mate, I need to …"

Tim chuckled. Dylan could see sheer relief all over his ruddy face. "I didn't reckon I'd be able to hold you back. Go. I've got someone coming in to relieve both of us. And, Knight?"

"Yeah?"

Tim's eyes welled. "Give her a big hug from me, will you?"

DYLAN PULLED UP at the Waters Gully football oval, a scene of many victories when he played in high school, and bolted towards what now resembled a camping ground. There were rows and rows of tents, in colours of taupe and bright blue and yellow, cars parked everywhere, barbecues sizzling away and ambulances and trucks and some young boys and girls kicking a football from one narrow end of the oval to the other up by the goal posts. There were clusters of adults milling around, some comforting others, some managing to find some humour in the dreadful experience they'd lived through, and others carrying young babies on their hips.

And there was a goat.

He knew instantly it was Zelda. She was tethered by a piece of bright orange cable to one of the tents and before he knew what he was doing, he was running as fast as his legs would carry him to that stupid head-butting goat. Because he knew that where Zelda was, he would find Hannie.

"Hannie?"

He stood outside the tent Zelda was attached to. From inside, there was a bark.

"Ted?"

"Dylan?"

"It's me."

"Dylan …"

He pulled open the tent flap. Hannie was on a blow up mattress lying flat on her back. Ted was at her side, his tail swiping happily. Dylan negotiated around the pile of mattresses on the floor of the tent and knelt at her side.

"Oh, god, Hannie. Are you okay?"

She didn't lift her head from the makeshift pillow of old towels which was jammed under her neck. "It's all gone."

He stroked her cheek, smoothed her hair away from her forehead. "I know. I went there looking for you."

Tears welled in her eyes. "How bad is it?" And then she gripped his hand. "Tell me the truth, Knight. I've already imagined the worst."

She was strong. She could handle this. "It's all gone, Hannie. I looked around to see if I could salvage anything precious. I found your jeweller's glasses. They're in my car. There's not much of them left."

Her lips wobbled. This brave woman was trying so hard to hold it all together. "And your place?"

He felt a pang of guilt. He paused and she knew why straight away.

"Tell me, Dylan? Your place? Is it okay?"

"It's fine. Yeah, it's fine. Fuck, Hannie. I thought you were… I was there and your car was parked out the front but I couldn't find you."

"Are you the one who told the police I was missing?" she whispered.

"I went looking for you. You weren't at home. You weren't at Uraidla. I thought…"

Her voice broke. "I was about to leave but Ted got out and I found him at the bottom of the creek bed. He's hurt his legs and he couldn't walk. So I tried to carry him up from the gully and that's when Mel and Kaz came and found me. That's when I hurt myself. They dragged Ted up to the car and me too. I was in no state to drive. That's why my car was still there. The ambos think I've slipped a disc."

It all made sense to Dylan now. He made a mental note to find a way to thank Mel and Kaz. If it wasn't for them… but he couldn't go down that rabbit hole again. Hannie was alive. She'd lost everything but she was alive. And he hadn't lost her.

A wave of emotion rose up in him and he didn't want to ignore it.

"I don't know what I would have done if…"

"Don't," she said abruptly, squeezing his hand. "Don't even go there. How am I going to tell my mum that I came that close? After all she's been through?"

"You're alive. That's what counts, Hannie. Thank god

you're alive."

Hannie wiped the tears from her eyes.

He studied her face. "God, I love you."

Her eyes widened. "I'm pretty doped up on drugs right now, but did you just say you love me?"

He leaned over, pressed his lips to hers. "Yeah, I do."

"You're not just saying that to distract me from what's happened?"

"No. The thought of losing you was… I was out of my mind. That's got to be love, right?"

She smiled and, thank god, she laughed, which then transformed into a shocked grimace. "Fuck," she murmured.

"Your back?"

She nodded. "When all this is over, I need to go to hospital."

He leaned in closer. "You do. I'm a first responder and I think that's the best course of treatment."

"But when I'm better, Dylan Knight, in about three months or a year, I'm going to jump your bones."

He pressed his lips to hers, gentle, sure, certain of his love for her. "I'm very much looking forward to that."

"Because I love you, too."

That was all he needed to hear. Carefully, he lay down on the grass next to the air mattress and reached for her hand. He didn't want to do anything that might bounce her around. She was in enough pain as it was.

"I have to get Ted to the vet, too."

"A dog needs to be able to walk."

"It could be his other knee. The vet did warn me that when one knee goes, the other isn't usually far behind."

"Poor, crippled up Ted," Dylan said. Ted licked his face. Dylan sucked it up. He figured Ted came with the package.

"And I'll have to find a new studio."

"Not too far away from Reynolds Ridge, I hope."

"I won't be going far."

"You can start again, right? Your skill is in your eye and what you see when you look at an old piece, in imagining what it can become."

"I managed to save some things. My smaller tools and all my stones. They're in the car. And the piece I made for my friend Beck, a few others."

Dylan squeezed her hand. "You're a smart woman."

"And I'll have to find somewhere to live. I've been lying here going over and over that particularly urgent dilemma."

Dylan pointed at the ceiling of the tent. "You might have to buy this thing. I'm sure you'll get a good price now that it's been used."

That was when they heard it. The sound of rain on the nylon fabric of the tent.

"Is that—" Hannie asked with a gasp.

"Yeah." Dylan propped himself up on an elbow. "It's raining." He kissed Hannie again.

"Ouch," she said. "Oh, there's one more thing. Zelda is going to need somewhere to live too."

Dylan ruminated on that one. "Okay, here's the deal. I'll only take Zelda if you come too. A package deal."

"Really?"

"Really."

"But we haven't even had a first date yet. And you're saying I can come stay with you?"

"Yeah. I'm that crazy about you, Reynolds."

She sighed and closed her eyes and Dylan watched her fall asleep, before he put his head on the rolled up towel next to hers and slept, too.

Chapter Eighteen

Hannie Reynolds and Dylan Knight's first date was a visit to the hospital emergency room.

The day after the fires were extinguished by soaking rains, he drove her into the city and she had a cortisone injection in her back to relieve the pressure on her disc. She hobbled in and hobbled slightly less on her way out.

Their second date was later that afternoon. They drove back up into the hills and to Reynolds Ridge to Dylan's place to pick up Ted to take him to the vet, where Hannie was told that, yes, Ted had torn the anterior cruciate ligament on his other knee and would need the same surgery. The vet kept him in overnight so she could do the surgery the next morning.

"A special favour," she'd told Hannie.

Hannie knew immediately what she meant. It was a special favour for someone who had just lost everything they owned in the bushfire.

Their third date was a trip to a suburban shopping centre so Hannie could buy knickers and shoes.

Their fourth date was a cold beer on Dylan's deck that night. In the fading evening light, they looked across the gully to the ruins of Mandy's property. It was strange to see the place in darkness.

Dylan checked his watch. "They should be here any minute."

Hannie nodded. Alice had called earlier, asking if they could come up and speak to Hannie. Of course she'd agreed, but suggested they head to Dylan's instead for their family meeting. Hannie hadn't been able to walk among the ruins of the cottage. She didn't think Mandy would be ready, either.

They heard Alice's car pull into the driveway and they put down their beers and walked around the back to the drive. Alice was helping Mandy out of the front passenger seat. When Mandy looked up, she beckoned Hannie over to her, and Hannie held out her arms and hugged her aunt. Only they knew what they'd shared on that property, and what they had lost.

"Hi, Hannie," Alice said stiffly. "Hello, Dylan."

"Come around onto the deck for a drink."

When they were all seated, Alice perhaps less comfortably than the others, she cleared her throat. "I don't think we need to beat around the bush."

Hannie looked at Dylan.

"No," Hannie said. She clenched her jaw, waiting for the onslaught. The difference, this time, was that she was prepared.

"Firstly," Alice said primly, "I just want to say, thank you Hannie for all you did to protect Mum's place."

"I did everything I could. I promise you."

"I know that, Hannie." Mandy looked up from her lap.

Hannie was shocked to see the difference in her aunt since she'd been away with Alice in the city, since her second fall. She seemed shrunken and little.

"I'm so sorry, Mandy. I had the sprinklers on. I'd checked the generators. Everything was cleared, even the gutters. I don't know what happened."

Dylan stretched an arm around Hannie's shoulders. "A bushfire happened. That's why the house and the cottage were destroyed."

"I don't blame you, Hannie. Don't forget, I grew up here too. I know what bushfires can do."

"I couldn't save the girls, Aunt Mandy. We didn't have room in the car for twenty chickens. But we rescued Zelda."

At the mention of her goat's name, Mandy broke into a smile. "Bloody Zelda."

"You're damn right about that," Dylan laughed. "She bleats all bloody night."

Dylan had broken the ice. They all laughed about Zelda, even Alice.

"And I need to apologise to you, Hannie," Mandy said. "I invited you to live in the cottage because I was scared of being on my own." Her voice faltered. "I'd already had the word from the doctors by then and I thought it would make me feel safer to have you around. I didn't think about what you might want for your own future. About your business."

Mandy looked up, wide-eyed. "How did you…"

"Your mother called me."

"I really was glad to help out." Hannie reassured her. "It was never a chore."

"But you have to get on with your own life. And there's something else I want you to know. I don't believe anything Alice has said. All this rubbish about free-loading and wanting a cut of my will. What a load of rot. I know the truth about you, Hannie. You have a big heart. My problem has always been that I've known the truth about my daughter and I haven't wanted to confront that."

Alice looked teary-eyed and guilty.

"We've been having some heart-to-heart conversations and I think Alice has something she wants to say."

Hannie and Dylan exchanged glances. He raised an eyebrow slightly in her direction.

"I'm sorry, Hannie. And I'm sorry, Dylan. For everything."

"We accept your apology," Dylan said. He turned to Mandy. "You're still going to sell up then?"

"Yes." She nodded. "Although it's land value now, maybe even less, given the cost of demolishing the house and the cottage, disconnecting all the electrical and the plumbing and so on. They're not safe the way they are and rebuilding would cost a fortune.

"That's someone else's adventure now," Mandy said. "I have good insurance so I'll be right."

"And what about you, Hannie?" Alice asked sheepishly. "What are you going to do?"

"I had contents insurance, and car insurance, and I've already spoken to the insurance company. Someone's coming out to do a site inspection in the next few days, so I'm hoping I'll have enough to replace all my jeweller's tools and furniture and stuff." She shrugged. "I'm looking at a space locally to set up a workshop and a retail space. Nothing I can confirm yet."

"So, I take it you're staying here with Dylan?"

"Yes. For a while, until I get things sorted out."

Dylan shot a glance at Hannie.

There was no reply from Alice. Hannie guessed it would take her a whole lot longer to feel happy for Hannie. She tried to figure out if she cared. She wasn't sure.

They shared a glass of wine and then Alice and Mandy decided it was time to leave. "We'll be back soon to have a look at the house in the daylight," Mandy said. "I'm still not ready." They walked as a group around to the back of the house to Alice's car. "If I don't see it in ruins, I can always keep that image in my mind's eye that it's still the same as it ever was. Do you know what I mean?"

"I do," Hannie said. "I understand exactly."

There was a final hug for Mandy before they left.

Dylan and Hannie collected the glasses and bottles from the deck and brought everything inside. While Dylan loaded the dishwasher, Hannie washed the wine glasses and stacked them in the draining rack.

Dylan locked the back door. Hannie turned out the lights, and they slowly walked hand in hand to the bedroom. They brushed their teeth in turn in the en suite, and when Hannie had taken the medication she'd been prescribed for her back, washed her face, and brushed her hair, she walked into the bedroom. Dylan was sitting on his side of the bed, shuffling through a pile of books on the bedside table.

She slipped off her sun dress and her shoes, slowly, ever conscious of the stabbing pain she feared might return as her back was healing. She pulled back the blanket on her side of the bed and slowly, painfully slowly, eased her legs into bed. She then lowered herself on her pillow.

Dylan reached over and pulled the covers over her.

"Thanks," she said ruefully. "I swear I'm going to make it up to you."

"Make what up?" Dylan got into bed and opened the pages of his novel.

"This sex drought. I can't believe it. We're in the prime of the first flush of love and romance and all that, when the sex is supposed to be smoking and adventurous and so damn hot we might melt, you know, in that phase before it becomes normal and regular and old married couple boring, and look at me. I can't do anything."

Dylan put his book down. "What do you mean 'old married couple boring'?"

"It's a figure of speech."

He hesitated. "You think you might want to, one day?"

Hannie waited. "To what one day?"

"Get married. Get old and boring with me."

Her heart beat fast in her chest. "Are you proposing, Dylan Knight?"

"Umm, I'm investigating."

"Keep asking questions then."

"Tonight, when Alice asked you if you were staying here with me, you said, 'Yeah for a while until you got things sorted out.' What things do you need to sort out?"

"My workshop. The rest of my life. You know, those things."

"The rest of your life is here with me. Haven't I made that perfectly fucking clear?"

"I need to know that we're still compatible sexually. What if all that hot sex we had before I hurt myself was just a fluke?"

"That's very important, to be compatible sexually," he said.

"Too bloody right," Hannie replied.

"I've got an idea." Dylan pulled the blankets from her body.

"What the hell are you doing?"

He moved down the bed. "You don't have to do anything. Just lie there." He skimmed a hand down her thigh and stopped. "If it doesn't hurt, can you move your legs?"

She parted them, slowly, her breath catching on her lips anticipating what was coming.

"That doesn't hurt?"

"No."

Dylan kissed her hip, the top of her thigh and then walked his fingers down, down, down, and teased her. "How's that?" he asked, his voice so sexy she almost came right on the spot.

"Not bad," she murmured.

"How about this?" He flicked her with his tongue and pressed down on her and she gasped.

"Better. Oh. Trying not to move here."

When he slipped his fingers inside her, her insides clenched and warmed and exploded.

After, Hannie decided that an orgasm was the best muscle relaxant ever invented.

Chapter Nineteen

T HREE MONTHS LATER, Hannie was well enough to live up to the promise she'd made to Dylan when they were lying in the tent at the Waters Gully evacuation centre during the bushfire.

She jumped his bones.

More than once, in fact.

It took a little while to recover, but all those weeks later she was back on her feet in more ways than one. Her life was moving forward in ways she had only dreamed about.

She now had a shopfront on the main road of Reynolds Ridge, thanks to Mel and Kaz. It turned out that they not only owned the shop that housed their organic cafe, but the whole building. They'd come to a fair arrangement for the rent and it was her workshop and retail space.

"It's a good fit," Mel had told her when she handed over the keys. "Our coffee and food, your jewellery, and if we're lucky, we'll entice a couple of other people to rent out the two other shops. We might even get the ridge back on the map."

The bushfires had scared people away, everyone knew that. It happened both ways. Some people left the hills and never came back, knowing they didn't have the mental strength to live through another fire that ferocious. For them, summers would always be a time of anxiety, not carefree days and nights. Others stayed away from the hills, even for lunches and trips to wineries, thinking they would let people recover.

Mel and Kaz and Hannie knew that the best way for people to get back on their feet was to have customers.

As it turned out, Mandy didn't end up demolishing the buildings on her property. Almost as soon as a new "For Sale" sign had been hammered into the ground by the local real estate agent, a couple from Adelaide, a builder and an interior designer, had driven by and decided on a hills change. Which was like a sea change but in the hills, they'd explained to Hannie and Dylan when they'd met at the cafe. They were planning to renovate the main house as a home for themselves and their three children and then rebuild Hannie's cottage as a bed and breakfast.

That made Mandy and Hannie very happy. When the sale had gone through, Mandy had moved into residential care. Hannie visited her every week. It really was a lovely facility and although Mandy had always painted herself as a loner who liked her singular life in the hills, she seemed to be enjoying new friendships with the other residents.

Hannie was still living at Dylan's and it was beginning to

feel more and more like her home every day. She felt so lucky that she didn't have to leave Reynolds Ridge, a place she'd loved since she was born. Every night, she sat out on Dylan's deck, looking out over the valley. As the weather turned, as summer became autumn and then winter, it rained and rained, soaking the scorched ground, and the burnt trees and shrubs all over the hills began to come back to life. New leaves sprouted, saplings grew, and flowers blossomed across the hills. It was one of nature's miracles in a landscape that had been singed into blackness just months before.

On his days off, Dylan had helped Hannie work on the interior of her shop. It needed some repairs and painting and together they'd transformed it into a beautiful retail space and studio. She'd found an old jeweller's desk online and with the insurance money she received for her car and contents, she had purchased tools and the things she needed to reestablish herself.

A month after the fire, when her back had settled enough for her to finally be able to drive again, Hannie went down to Semaphore and presented Beck with the reimagined piece of jewellery.

Hannie had passed Beck a small white box and then waited. She loved presenting her pieces to clients this way. It made the moment more important. It somehow made them stop and wonder and guess about what was inside, it heightened their excitement about what was to be revealed and it gave Hannie a little moment to think about how much she loved the art of creating.

When Beck flipped the box open, she gasped and covered her mouth with a hand.

"Oh, Hannie," she'd whispered. "It's just absolutely perfect." Three hearts, three diamonds, joined together forever. That was grandmother, mother and daughter. Beck had hugged her so hard, and Hannie knew it wasn't just for the brooch. It was for all Hannie had lost in the fire.

Ted had come home after a couple of nights at the vets and since then, with two new knees, he was an unstoppable, slobbering muddy hound. With the autumn and winter rains filling the creek, he was never more at home than when he was in it, and Dylan had almost stopped complaining about the muddy paw prints throughout the house.

As for Dylan, they made up for lost time. They were still heavily into the first flush of love and romance and all that, and the sex was smoking and adventurous and so damn hot they did melt. Hannie was still waiting for it to become normal and regular and old married couple boring, but that seemed a long way off given the way he looked at her. Like she was the only woman in the world.

And, with each day that passed, she loved him more.

On this particular day, she was in her workshop, sketching out designs on a new piece she'd just won a commission for. Beck had shown someone the brooch Hannie had made and that someone had mentioned it to a neighbour who had contacted Hannie. For her, word of mouth was the best way to win business. Recommendations from the heart meant so much more to her. She was leaning over her sketch pad, drawing small circles and bigger ones, looking at the space between each and how the shapes might combine.

The bell above the front door to her shop rang and she looked up.

How was it that her heart still went crazy when she saw him?

"Hey," Dylan said.

He walked through the shop, past the display she had set up with small pieces she'd made to give people an idea of what she could do, and came back to the rear, where her work space was set up. He was carrying a brown paper bag.

She looked up to him and he leaned down and smiled before kissing her.

"What are you working on?" He looked over her shoulder.

"Just ideas at this stage. I'm trying to see if something catches hold." She nodded at the brown paper bag in his hand. "What's that?"

"An apple muffin from next door."

"Is that for me?"

He handed it over with a smile.

"You know thinking makes me hungry." Hannie opened the bag and sniffed the deliciously scent of it, apple and cinnamon and butter and brown sugar. "Mel and Kaz are amazing."

"They sure are," Dylan said.

Hannie looked up at him and noticed something was off. He seemed kind of serious or hesitant about something.

"You all right?" She put the bag on her desk and reached for his hand. She tugged him closer and slipped her arms around his thigh.

"Yeah. I'm good. It's just that…" He stepped back from her so he could dig a hand into the one of the pockets of his jeans.

He looked at Hannie solemnly. "I need your advice about something."

"Sure. About what?"

He put a hand between them, flipped it over and opened his flingers. There was a ring in the middle of his palm.

"Oh my god. That is gorgeous." Hannie picked it up and held it up to the light. She reached for her new jeweller's glasses and slipped them on. "This is a stunning piece. It looks early twentieth century and that is a beautiful red ruby sitting right in the middle there. I'd say it's maybe half a carat. A gold setting. And, all around it, see here?" She ran a gentle finger around the gem. "They're white Swiss-cut diamonds." She slipped off her glasses and put them on her desk. "It's beautiful, Dylan."

She went to hand it back to him but his hands were in his pockets.

"You think you could do something with that?" he

asked.

She blanched. "You've got to be kidding. I'm not touching that. It's absolutely perfect as it is."

"And so are you." Dylan took the ring back and reached for her hand, urging her to stand.

"What are you doing?"

"Hannie Reynolds, will you marry me?"

"Oh, my god." She gasped. "That's an engagement ring? That beautiful thing you're holding?"

Dylan chuckled. "Yeah, that's what I was thinking. But I was hedging my bets in case you didn't like it. You're an expert in this stuff and I didn't want to get you something you thought was ugly."

"It's not ugly. It's magnificent." She began to cry.

"Come on now." Dylan pulled her close, held her tight, wrapped her up in his love and held her close to his heart, a place she wanted to be forever.

Hannie let her tears flow. How could she explain to Dylan that she was crying for everything she'd been through in the past four months? The troubles with Alice, Ted, the bushfires, losing her home, finding a new one, and finding such a strong love in the midst of all that? Life had thrown her up into the air like a kite and she'd landed someplace good.

Better than good. Wonderful.

She took a deep breath and pulled back a little she could show him how happy she was. "Yes, Knight. I'd love to marry you."

Then he laughed and there were tears in his eyes, too. "Do you have any idea of the pressure I was under? What if you hated it? What if I'd chosen something butt ugly, which had turned out to be cubic zirconia and not diamonds?"

She kissed him. "I still would have said yes."

He kissed her right back, full of love and joy and promises about a future they would share together.

She slipped on the ring. It gleamed on her finger like a constellation of stars in the night sky. It was a little tight but she could fix that easily.

"I'm so glad you came home, Knight."

"Me, too, Reynolds."

Dylan reached for her hand and kissed the back of it. Hannie didn't know how it was possible to be happier than she'd been the past few months, but she was.

She might have lost all her possessions in the fire, but she'd found something so much more important.

She still had Ted. She had this new life.

And she had found the love of her life.

Her heart was right here in Reynolds Ridge where it belonged.

The End

The Hot Aussie Knights

Headed by grandfather Leonard (The Legend) Knight, the Knight family is fire-fighting royalty in Australia. Two generations have followed in Leonard's highly distinguished footsteps and nowadays, despite being scattered across the length and breadth of Australia, it's the five Knight cousins who keep the Hot Aussie Knight legacy alive, working hard and playing hard, day and night.

Book 1: *Hot Mess* by Amy Andrews

Book 2: *Burning Both Ends* by Sinclair Jayne

Book 3: *Long Hot Summer* by Victoria Purman

Book 4: *Burning Love* by Trish Morey

Available now at your favorite online retailer!

About the Author

Award-nominated and multi-published Australian contemporary romance author Victoria Purman loves books, wine, chocolate, sad country music, hard rock songs and stories with happy ever afters. Writing romance means she regularly gets to indulge in all those things – as well as being forced into online pictorial research for her emotional, funny and smart love stories. In 2014, Victoria was a finalist in the RuBY Awards (the Romance Writers of Australia's "Romantic Book of the Year" Awards) for the first book on her Boys of Summer series for Harlequin MIRA, Nobody But Him. That same year, she was named a finalist in the category "Favourite New Author 2013" by the Australian Romance Readers Association. Most days, she considers herself the luckiest woman in the world.

Visit her website at VictoriaPurman.com

Thank you for reading

Long Hot Summer

If you enjoyed this book, you can find more from all our great authors at TulePublishing.com, or from your favorite online retailer.

TULE
PUBLISHING

Printed in Great Britain
by Amazon

35156354R00132